flashlite Lattures

823
B39n

NO SECOND SPRING

NO SECOND SPRING

A Novel

BY

JANET BEITH

FREDERICK A. STOKES COMPANY

NEW YORK   MCMXXXIII

Printed in the United States of America

To
F. P. B

"But the broken heart it kens
No second spring again,
Tho' the waefu' may cease frae
their greetin'."

Scots Air

NO SECOND SPRING

PROLOGUE

THE family portraits that hung on the dining-room wall were framed in dull gold. They could not be moved because the wallpaper had faded so much behind them. They had hung in the same places for twenty years.

They were gloomy black-coated individuals, these nineteenth century McGregor ancestors. Here and there appeared a yellow waistcoat or a spotted cravat, but nothing more startling than this broke the monotony of the grays and blacks.

There were two or three portraits of the Very Rev. Hamish Quentin McGregor, D.D., great-grandfather of the present generation; these were all forbidding in appearance. There was, however, a hint of excitement in the expression of the earliest portrait, painted in Eighteen-thirty-two. In this, Hamish Quentin had a vast head of brown hair, short side-whiskers, and clear gray eyes. He wore a high white stock beneath a Byronic collar. One of the most outstanding features of the picture was the blue-veined, beautifully shaped hand.

Among the portraits of these somber ancestors hung one of a woman. It arrested attention among the others because of its lightness; it was unfinished.

The background had a thin layer of paint, and only the face was completed. It was unsigned, but printed on the dull gold frame in small black letters was the following inscription:

Allison Chisolm, wife of the Very Rev. Hamish
McGregor, D.D.
1832

So this was the famous minister's wife, mother of ten children, according to the family tree. In the portrait she seemed little more than a child. She was clad in black with a lace fichu, and her hair was dark and soft. A gentle happiness seemed to radiate from the large and beautiful eyes.

Why was it that the light of happiness shone so clearly from the face in the unfinished portrait? Was life in an out-of-the-way Highland Parish so joyous? What was it like to look forward to years of constant child-bearing?

There was another problem attached to the portrait. Why was it not completed? The companion portrait of the minister, painted presumably by the same artist, was perfectly finished.

It seemed as though the portrait of the woman had been left off suddenly; there were careless brush marks in the corners, as though the artist had wiped his brush there thoughtlessly.

The minister's portrait was signed with initials only, "A.S." No one had succeeded in identifying this "A.S." The picture seemed the work of an inexperienced artist, careless in technique, but there was a life about the woman's face which never failed to attract attention. Often there was a question on the lips of the idle spectator.

CHAPTER I

THE noise of the wind was a perpetual torture. The snow-flakes floated past in bewildering masses. Allison watched them in a numbed trance, following them with her tired eyes, as they sifted across the yellow circle of light which was thrown from the gig's lamp. She watched them till they disappeared suddenly, swallowed up by the shrieking, battling darkness, then she dragged her wearied gaze back to the other side of the circle of light, and followed the silent hurry of the snow again.

The snow, which lay thickly at the sides of the road, seemed to her to unroll before them, as they moved forward by the light of one flickering lamp.

There was no sound from the clogged hooves of Paddy, no sound from the wheels of the gig as they passed over the softness of the snow.

Allison tore her eyes from their insane pursuit of the snow-flakes; for the last half-hour she had felt that she was no longer a living in-

4

dividual, but some machine set there to follow the course of that ceaseless drifting.

The gig-lamp threw a strange glinting light along the plodding back of old Paddy, a cloud of vapor rose from his flanks. Allison noticed how the snow lay in a smooth enlarged semblance of the harness-straps, obscuring the hardness of the buckles; every now and then the horse shook his head and a shower of thin frozen snow was scattered from his shaggy mane.

She cowered towards Hamish as a fiercer blast than usual met the struggling gig round a bend in the road. Paddy hesitated in his mechanical plodding. She shuddered, but said nothing.

Hamish's hands in their rough sheepskin gauntlets fascinated her. She was so tired that it seemed impossible to uproot her gaze from any object upon which it had alighted. She heard him encourage the bewildered horse; the full slow tones of his voice seemed to be torn away from his lips and hurled into the abyss of darkness beyond the orange circle of the lamp.

He urged Paddy gently with the reins, touching him on the back with his numbed fingers. Still the horse would not, or could not, move;

he stood there, the snow piled almost to his knees and the soft flakes settling secretly along his back.

Hamish leaned down so that his mouth was opposite to Allison's ear. She felt the strength of his arm round her shoulders, and smelt the friendly smell of the wet tweed cape. She felt the cold touch of his thick brown hair, as the wind plucked it ruthlessly from the circle of his head.

"I must get down and lead him, Allison; the snow's deeper here, and the beast will not go on alone."

She nodded her head slowly, although she had not fully realized the import of his words. She wished he would stay there that she might rest her head on his shoulder, and hide her stinging, cringing hands beneath the folds of his great cape. Her face was in the shadow, but something in the dejected droop of her slight shoulders, weighed down by the vast plaid in which they were wrapped, arrested his eagerly working brain for a moment. He drew her close to him again and spoke into her ear.

"Be strong, Allison," he murmured, in that musical voice which always had the power to stir her; "we cannot be far from the Inn at

Neabost, where there'll be warmth and food."

For a second Allison's numbness deserted her and with it her accustomed calm. She clung to him, beseeching him not to climb down into the snow, leaving her alone to battle with the torture of the wind and those dreadful ceaseless snow-flakes. Tears of sheer fatigue ran down her cheeks, as she implored him with eyes and tongue to stay by her side.

For a moment his grasp tightened round her shoulders, but a glance at the gathering snow on Paddy's back brought him to his senses with a jerk. Gently but firmly he disengaged himself from her clinging fingers.

"Allison—Allison," he said reproachfully. "Where is your strength? The snow is gathering, and if we are to reach the Inn we must go on while we can." Her fingers still clung desperately to his cape. His eye caught sight of the growing snow-drifts at the side of the road, and then wandered to the vast shrieking darkness round them.

He and Allison were two infinitesimal atoms, swamped and overwhelmed by an unknown ancient power. He felt the strength of that primeval country surging through the darkness, grinning at him from the light-splashed snow round the gig. Bewildered by thoughts which he hardly dared to pursue, he glanced once more at the pathetic oval of Allison's face.

"It is the Lord's will, my dear; the Lord will provide." This must be the answer to that feeling of desolation that had swept over him, a feeling of himself as an atom, a mere nothing in some vast organization. Allison's fingers released their grasp. She knew that she could hold him no longer; she felt the resolution which had made him withdraw his arm.

He clambered down into the snow, his footmarks making clumsy black caverns in the unbroken smoothness. With the strength and gentleness of his hand he urged the exhausted and faltering beast forward. Very slowly the gig proceeded, Allison swaying cruelly with every jolt of the wheels. She had closed her eyes now; she could not bear the sight of those hurrying snow-flakes any longer. "The Lord's will be done," she muttered over and over again to herself. It meant nothing to her; it was a mere string of sounds which seemed to ring in her ears, the last sounds which had broken the monotony of the noise of the wind in the hollows of the mountains.

She thought about the two children follow-

ing behind in the farm cart with Bella and
John. She had wanted to take them with her
in the gig, but Hamish had been adamant. She
shuddered when she thought of their cold and
hunger; she screwed up her eyes in horror and
clenched her fists; the snow-flakes seemed to be
dashing before her eyes again and settling
quietly, furtively, in the soft red curls of her
children. She must not think any more about
them. Hamish had said that the Lord would
provide. "The Lord's will be done," she murmured again.

Then quite suddenly, she thought, "It cannot be the Lord's will; it is the storm's will, it
is the will of all these vast, these terrible, mountains, it is the will of this creeping, silent snow."
She opened her eyes, terrified. It could not be
the Lord's will to freeze her children to death,
to leave her sitting in a gig, swaying madly from
side to side, a butt for every shrieking, insult-
ing blast. "The Lord is merciful and of loving
kindness," she thought wildly, blotting out the
picture of the snow creeping over the two small
creatures following in the farm cart. The snow
was unreal, the cold and the tumultuous darkness were unreal; they did not exist; only the
rounded limbs and the color of Alex's hair, and

the sound of the children's voices were real. Surely the unreal could not creep over the real until it did not exist. The Lord would fight against the dreadful influence that streamed from the hills, terrifying in its relentless force. Then there crept into her mind the realization that the power of the storm was the strength of the Lord Himself; was He not the maker of storms? Could He not command the elements? "Peace be still."

But the storm was hostile, mocking at the puny mortals that struggled across the face of the earth. A real terror began to grip the mind of Allison; she gave a little cry and stretched out her hand towards Hamish. But he did not hear; he plodded doggedly ahead, the snow clinging to his cape, and to the thickness of his hair.

He lifted his feet mechanically out of the depth of the snow; he was like a machine.

His brain was filled with thoughts which tumbled one over the other, jumbled together because of his weariness. He thought chiefly of the distance that divided them from the Neabost Inn, then his mind swung back and he saw again Allison's frightened eyes as she had begged him to stay with her in the gig. She had acted like a frightened child, and yet, he ruminated, she was twenty-four years of age, the mother of two children, the mistress of his Manse for over six years. He had not seen her like this since the night that Alex was lost in the woods above Kolbrocher; for a moment the settled calm of his mind was ruffled. What a strange glance she had given him when he had assured her with the name and promise of the Lord; but then perhaps she was not quite in her usual frame of mind; the third baby should be born in—he counted up on his fingers—in about six weeks he thought—he had to count twice to make quite sure.

Marriage was primarily for the procreation of children. The process had at first been made golden for him by a sort of mystic light shining on it; the first time he had gazed down on the strange yet moving features of a child of his own, he had been stirred by the immense wonder of it. He had gloried in the magnificent secret power which lay in his manhood, a power which could create a new intelligence, a living microcosm which had its own entity and had never been before, and would never be again. By a series of logical steps he had reduced this sensation of a life-pulse within him to an inherent awe of what he termed "The Living God." Hamish liked to have his sensations clear, he liked to know what had given rise to them. Sometimes he was puzzled and therefore a little angry, but usually he could fit in his sensations to his creed.

Marriage was for the procreation of children; the Scriptures said so. He had been glad of that when he had felt that surge of power which he had experienced when he gazed down upon his first offspring. It was highly satisfactory that such a pleasant thing should be in accordance with the Scriptures, for the God of Hamish was a hard, relentless God. Pleasure was irretrievably linked with vice in the mind of the young minister.

This was to be his third offspring. The process of inspecting the newly-borns was losing its particular pleasure. It would have been easy enough to feel again the surge of wonder and pleasure that had accompanied the first sight of a child of his own creating. He could have re-experienced it perhaps half a dozen times with an almost equal freshness, if it had not been that his mind wandered with such certainty into the future, robbing the present of its rightful pleasure. Stretched out before him, he saw an indefinable stream of young McGregors, and as he gazed down on the head of the newly-born baby, he could not help but feel that it was, after all, only one in many. He had found himself thinking this as he had inspected his second offspring. At the thought of the third addition to his family, he merely felt a kind of warm satisfaction, as though part of his task for the year was about to be successfully concluded.

Thoughts of this nature pursued their way indefinitely across the field of Hamish's brain, as he urged Paddy onward through the snow, holding the lantern out so that it threw its circle of light before the horse's feet.

The lights of the Inn drew nearer and nearer as the gig jogged drunkenly onwards. They crossed a bridge at the bottom of the hill, the horse's hooves thudding hollowly over the temporary beams of which it was composed.

The Neabost Inn stood to the left of the road. The snow lay a foot deep round about and the grim dilapidated walls and roof were rounded and softened by it. Lights streamed through the bottom windows, and the sound of voices could be heard even above the shriek of the wind.

Hamish approached the door, lantern in hand. The snow was trodden to a muddy brown round the doorway. In vain he knocked; the noise of the angry wind without and the upraised voices within drowned his efforts. Then the skirl of the pipes was added to the uproar, the weird notes rising high above the crash of the storm.

At last, his patience exhausted, Hamish put his shoulder to the door and brought his great weight to bear against it. It burst open with a sudden rush, precipitating him within. He stood in the doorway regarding the scene, the snow-flakes swirling in behind him, settling on his black cape.

The room inside was bare and dismal, the floor seemed little more than beaten mud, the windows were patched and plugged with dirty rags which fluttered in the draught. The fireplace was sunk in the wall and the thick acrid peat-smoke swept forward into the room in a bellying cloud, as the wind rushed in through the open door. There was a table bearing drinking-vessels, and several rough benches, but no other furniture. The men, gathered round the fire, coughed and cursed as the smoke was swirled into their eyes and throats. The host rose unsteadily to his feet, a red-headed man smelling vilely of whisky and peat-smoke. He advanced towards the young minister, swearing at him in Gaelic, and wrenched the door shut again.

Hamish, standing inside, dazed by the light of two lamps which swung from the beams, leaned against the walls for a moment speechless. Then he demanded lodging and food for his family. His Gaelic was quiet and faultless; the innkeeper was visibly impressed, although he maintained that he had no other accommodation except that which was offered by the room which lay before him. However, when Hamish explained that he was the new minister for Glenlee, and that he had his wife with him, the man, now sullenly civil, bade him follow up a creaking uncarpeted stair, which led to an upper room. The room was cold and running with damp and had one bed, but it was better than nothing; in it privacy would at least be enjoyed.

The minister descended and, tearing open the door once more, he bore the acquiescent, almost unconscious Allison over the threshold and up the dark unfriendly stairs. He laid her gently on the bed. She lay like a tired child, utterly inert.

"I must go back over the road and help John with the cart," he told her. She opened her eyes, startled; the thought of the cart still open to the snow and the screech of the storm had faded from her mind; with a sickening wave all her anxieties returned, her two babies—with fluttering fingers she urged him to be gone.

"You are not afraid, Allison?" he inquired, beating his numbed hands together as he prepared to leave her. "We should all be back soon—the cart cannot be far behind us on the road. The men below-stairs are only drovers returning to the Islands; they will not bother you—they have other attractions." He added this grimly; he had seen the gleam of the lamplight on bottles of yellow liquid.

He closed the door and left her lying on the damp musty coverlet. The wind whispered round the room, creeping in through a broken pane. The candle guttered and streamed in the draught, throwing splashes of light along the dusty walls, revealing long bleared streaks where the damp had made its way over their surface.

Allison lay so still that she might have been

part of that silent, lifeless apartment. Her eyes were shut, but the snow-flakes still seemed to be chasing each other stealthily across her field of vision in an endless hurrying flock.

Presently she roused herself; leaning on her elbow she looked about her. Slowly she lowered her feet to the ground. She thought mechanically that she must prepare the room for the children. The fireplace contained a pile of chips and other rubbish, a stack of untidy peats leaned against the wall.

She went down on her knees and rearranged the damp chips. She was so cold that her fingers could hardly grasp the fragments of wood. She set a light to the pile by means of the candle. Twice the blue smoke curled upwards and died away. She could hear the hiss of water as it oozed from some of the larger chips. At the third effort the smaller scraps of wood began to light, and soon the whole mass was smoldering in a gloomy way. At every onset of the storm a rush of wind swept down the chimney, sending puffs of blue smoke out into the room.

Allison rose slowly. She felt giddy and her feet were like frozen blocks of ice. It was such a little time till the birth of her baby, and it made her tired and helpless. Tears rose to her brown eyes. Hamish would have to do it all; she could not even light the fire without clouds of thick choking smoke filling the room. It had always been his cry that she was "feckless," unable to fend for herself. She had heard him protest so often that human beings were not eggshells. "If you're not afraid of things," he had said to her just after they were married, "then the things scarcely exist." She wondered if there was anything that he feared. Those gray eyes of his were like two challenging steel weapons confronting the world; and then he seemed to know so much about God, as though he were in the Divine confidence; with what ease and assurance he would produce his, "The Lord's will be done," and the fatal, "The Lord will provide." How was it that he knew so much about the Lord?

Ashamed and horror-struck at her own weakness, Allison crept slowly towards the bed. She turned back the coverlet. There were spots of damp on the sheets, and, much worse, two large gray bugs. She started back dismayed. It was infested. She replaced the coverlet hastily and stood with her hand pressed to her aching forehead; it was all like a bad dream—

the thick choking atmosphere, the crawling damp bed, the rising voices of the men accompanied by the skirl of pipes in the room below. She crouched by the smoldering peats, the plaid wrapped round her; thus she fell asleep.

Chapter II

Hamish returned along the snow-clad road on foot, having first led the exhausted Paddy into the stable at the back of the Inn. The storm was, if anything, fiercer than it had been when Allison and he had descended the hill a quarter of an hour earlier. The snow stung against his cheek and the wind seemed to pierce through his black homespun clothes; he had left his cape over Paddy to serve as some sort of shield against the damp and draught of the inadequate stable. He toiled up the hill and over the bridge, clinging to the rickety rail, as the wind met him with its full force.

But Hamish was enjoying himself. He loved that feeling of power which a battling with adverse circumstances always brought to him; he gloried in the strength of an intellect which could lift anything as puny as a man above the enormous forces of nature and adversity. There was nothing he hated so much as the feeling of himself as an impotent atom in the diurnal course of the world.   He felt himself to be Man with a capital M; gifted with a divine spirit, he could triumph over every other force except the force of the God he worshiped, this God who had created the world merely as a background for divine creatures of his own workmanship.   Earlier in the night Hamish had felt the overwhelming power of the storm and he had turned from it, secretly afraid.   But now, as he toiled up the hillside, his spirits rose higher and higher; once or twice he hummed to himself.   The wind became stronger as he neared the point where the road winds round the corner of the hill, and he settled down to a rhythmical plodding, his steps keeping time to the lilt of a Gaelic rowing song which beat insistently in his head.   The sleet seemed to be stripping the skin from his face, and he often stumbled, half blinded by its force.

At last he saw the light of the cart a hundred yards ahead of him.   He halted and, panting with his exertions, stood stamping his feet on the snow-clad road.   Presently it drew level with him and he hailed it eagerly.

John led the heavy, thick-maned beast; both man and horse were completely whitened by the driving snow.   As Hamish spoke to him

he could see the water streaming off his rugged
cheeks, and the snow clinging to his thick griz-
zled eyebrows and whiskers, as the light from
the lamp caught his face. In the cart behind
sat Bella, wrapped in a dark plaid. The two
children lay close against her; they both slept
peacefully. Hamish caught a glimpse of Alex's
face, but Bella would not move to let him see
Jean; the old servant sat there frozen with cold,
worn out with fatigue, but her face still wore
its habitual expression of slightly ironical con-
tempt for the poor "feckless" bodies that inhabited this earth.

"Get awa' on, man," she said shrilly, addressing John, who, although cold and weary, was
glad of a chance to cease his heavy plodding
for a moment.

Hamish said nothing; the presence of Bella
always gave him a slightly uncomfortable feeling, as though a pin had been plunged into the
balloon of his self-esteem. She was a lowland
Scot of the most uncompromising type; her
motto through life had been, "If ye'r wantin' a
thing done properly, do it yersel'." The sloth
and ineptitude of other people filled her with
disdain. Hidden away beneath her rather
dour exterior was a grim sense of humor, which

sometimes troubled Hamish; he could not bring himself to believe that she was laughing at him, but occasionally he had suspected that she did not regard him with the respect due to him. When he was not present, however, she extolled him to her neighbors as the paragon of all human virtues; if her minister had faults, no one should know it. She regarded this move to the Highlands as an unparalleled piece of lunacy, and during all her stay at Glenlee she could never bring herself to consider the Highland people as more than dirty, drunken, ignorant bodies. There was always a hint of a sniff in her voice when she spoke of them.

Hamish watched the horse strain forward; with a jerk the cart lurched onward and they began to descend the hill.

Once or twice he addressed remarks to Bella, who answered him shortly, brooding over her injuries; that she, a God-fearing woman of Minniegaff in the Stewartry, should be dragged through godless Highland hills in a snowstorm seemed incredible. As she thought this she drew the plaids closer round the children, and her rough horny hands were gentle. Thus

Hamish found some difficulty in keeping the conversational ball rolling.

Arrived once more at the Inn, Hamish burst open the door again, which screeched as it forced its warped way over the flagstone floor. With a child held firmly on either arm, he strode into the kitchen, followed by the half-frozen, but unbowed, Bella.

The noise had risen to a tumult and the pipes screeched discordantly. The supply in the yellow bottles was begining to run low. The minister hesitated a moment, glancing at the "wag at the wa'" clock, which registered ten minutes before midnight, ten minutes till the Sabbath dawned. The light of battle sprang to his tired eyes. He would celebrate his first night in his own parish (even if it was only the outskirts of it) by a triumph: the people he had come to live amongst should see with what kind of man they had to deal. A glow set up in his weary numbed limbs, and he strode across the kitchen towards the staircase with renewed vigor.

He threw open the door of the bedroom forcibly, holding the children together on his other arm.

It was almost dark within, and smoke eddied

forth into his face, making him cough. The smell of damp and dust assailed his nostrils. The candle stood on a broken chair, throwing a dim shivering circle of yellow light. Allison slept in a huddled heap by the hearthside.

He laid the children on the bed and strode towards her. This was hardly the place he expected to find his wife, sleeping on the floor like any shepherd's dog. He bent down and tapped her sharply on the shoulder. She awoke with a quick startled cry, looking up into his face bewildered. When she saw who it was, her little hands fluttered towards him joyfully, and the plaid fell from round her shoulders. Her soft dark hair curled untidily about her face, and she looked so much of a child gazing up at him that he had not the heart to scold her.

"Allison," he said gently, "you should not be sitting on the floor, my dear; it is draughty and cold—your hair is all loosed on your shoulders."

With nervous fingers she sought to restrain her offending tresses, looking up at him with scared eyes, a blush creeping slowly over her white face.

"The children are here," Hamish continued

with a change of tone, as he prodded the dismal peats with his foot.

Allison struggled to her feet and, tired and stiff as she was, hurried across the room to where the babies lay. Jean, the elder child, was sitting up on the bed, her wide gray eyes wandering apprehensively round the grimness of the room. Alex still slept, his head buried in the damp mustiness of the coverlet.

In a moment Allison was on her knees by the bed, her arms encircling the two children, her hands playing with their hair, her mouth seeking the softness of their baby necks. She murmured eagerly to them, drawing them towards her.

She was startled by the sound of a crash, and the thickening of the smoke. Hamish, with his excessive manly touch, had been too forceful for the antiquity of the fireplace; the grate now sprawled drunkenly forward in a broken mass, while smoldering peats filled the air with choking blue smoke. He stood above the wreckage, ruefully regarding the damage. His face was smeared with black from his hands; he held a twisted poker. It is strange that the misplacement of an object from its natural setting should almost invariably produce the ludicrous. Thus the presence of peat on Hamish's cheek-bones appeared ludicrous and illuminating to Allison, whereas in its natural setting of the fireplace it had appeared unremarkable and even loathsome. Hamish no longer stood before her as that intangible spirit that set the standard, and marked the circumference of her existence; he was no longer the inspired minister of the gospel, with eyes that challenged the world and the unbeliever; he was simply a ludicrous figure, almost pathetic in his impotence.

She hurried across to his assistance, smiling up at him, her fatigue forgotten for the moment. She wrestled with the blackened iron with her small firm hands, while he knelt beside her assisting and hindering her with his presence. She laid her smudged little hand upon his shoulder to assist herself to rise; for a moment Hamish forgot the various purposes that had been surging through his active brain, his ideas for righting the fireplace, his intention of quietening the drunken brawl beneath —he thought only of Allison and the gentleness in the touch of her hand upon his shoulder. He did not think of her deeply, but the warmth and companionship of her presence was a pleasant sensation to him which he did not trouble to analyze. She saw the passive homage in his eyes and thrilled to it. It was so seldom that she felt herself to be worthy of this great husband of hers, whose mind seemed to be an ever-burning flame, who could see so clearly into the misty uncertain places of thought that left her either bewildered or terrified. She hesitated a moment before withdrawing her hand. Perhaps he was in love with her still; he had been once; she had seen the flame in him flicker with the zeal of something more primitive and fundamental than the canons of right and wrong which fed the flame of his spirit now; but then, of course, they had been married six years, and married people were not in love with one another—not in the way that she meant. Joy surged into her tired brain; nothing much seemed to matter to her now: her babies were safe, and Hamish loved her, she felt sure of it from the expression of his face—and then the monotonous striking of the clock in the parlor below rose above the clamor of voices. It struck twelve doggedly and insistently.

In a moment the Hamish that she glimpsed very occasionally and who had come to be considered by her almost as a dream phantom of her own brain, seemed to fade, the light in his eyes blazed brighter, but she knew that he was no longer aware of her individuality or of her femininity. His eager brain was once more on its swerveless way.

"It is the Lord's day," he said in a low tone, almost as though he were speaking to himself. He rose abruptly to his feet, wiping the smuts from his face with his handkerchief.

"I shall not be long, my dear," he said to Allison as he walked across the creaking boards towards the door.

"You're not going down among those men, Hamish?" she faltered, a quick fear settling over her recent spell of pleasure. "Oh, Hamish, they don't know you, they will not stop at your bidding, they're cruel and out of their senses, wild men from the Islands—don't go down amongst them—call to them from the stairway." She stood before him looking up at him eagerly from her small height.

He threw open the door and the sudden surge of voices burst into the room. "I should have a fair chance shouting from the stairway above that clamor," he said scornfully. "It is my duty, Allison; they will do me no harm. I am their

minister and they know it." Hamish was enjoying the moment; he felt spectacular, like
some carved image of valor; he knew that both
his wife, and he hoped Bella, were regarding
him with a mixture of terror and admiration.
A filthy oath broke in upon his words and he
heard the sound of men struggling together and
the crash of falling bottles. In a moment the
vision of himself as a carved statue of valor
vanished from his brain; he was not conscious
of himself now, only of that hard and fast
round of ideals that he had set up under the
heading "The Will of God." He stepped out
into the passage and slowly descended the stairs.

The men in the room below were in various
stages of intoxication, some of them sprawled
on the settle by the fireside, whilst some slept
like dogs curled on the floor. A vast red-headed
giant was struggling with a thick-set man,
whose drunken strength was invincible. An
audience of five or six men and one or two
women applauded and encouraged, sitting on
a long wooden bench.

Hamish stood in the doorway in silence.
The scene stamped itself irremovably on his
memory. His eyes dwelt idly on the drunken
face of a boy, who lay with his head in the crook

of his arm; the imbecile blankness of the face seemed pitiful in that thick lurid atmosphere. The light of the lamps caught the glass of the bottles, so that they gleamed and shone where they stood in the dark corners of the room; the lights on them moved with the shadows cast by the struggling men.

A madness seemed to enter into Hamish; the white flesh of the red-haired giant, which showed through a great rent in his shirt, seemed something hateful and degraded to him, and the sly stupidity in the drunken face of the sleeping boy a foul contagion, fighting against the fierceness and cleanness of life as it should be lived.

He ran into the room, his powerful musical voice harsh with anger. They heard him and paused in their struggle. He stood before them, his face white with fatigue, and a cold collected anger in his voice that crept, like a trickle of icy water, into the hot blurred brains of the drunken men. Words seemed to pour from his lips in a sharp clear current. He commanded them to desist, and then upbraided them for their desecration of the Sabbath. All the time he was aware of the cunning blankness of the face of the sleeping boy, so that somehow his voice trembled. An overwhelming sense of pity suddenly swept over him; the caressing light lingered on the mighty contours of the combatants, lingering fitfully on the magnificent shape of a shoulder or a thigh, and gleaming on the thick thatch of hair. The strength that shone in the eyes of the fighters seemed to be something born of the storm outside, it had the same intangible might. The sense of all this beauty wasted, tore at the mind of the young minister; somewhere behind the eyes which shone in the faces of these men there must be the white flame, the immortal soul.

They stood regarding him with hostility; he had held them silent for a moment or two, his intellect towering for a short space over their burning animal spirits, but now they crowded angrily round him, growling and murmuring in Gaelic. Slowly he was driven back towards the door. With a sudden thrust they sent him flying into the passage, slamming the door shut which divided the stairs from the parlor.

Hamish stood there in the dark, the blood surging in his ears. He had heard the bolt shot on the other side; it would be useless to attempt to re-enter. Slowly he turned and mounted the stairs. He had failed in his first attempt to quell his people in the name of the Lord; it was not the failure that ate into his flesh, but an indefinable fear of some unknown power. The power that he had felt in the strength of the snow, and which he had seen burning in the eyes of the beautiful red-haired giant. It was the power of an age-old Earth, that took no heed of the struggles of mankind to escape, that offered no comfort beyond that of the presence of the Earth itself.

Hamish entered the bedroom, where his wife was waiting for him, her face strained and white with listening. He did not answer her eager questions and soon she desisted, afraid of his displeasure.

The candle was burnt right down and the wick floated in a sea of melted wax; the flame lengthened and blobbed, casting weird shadows on the damp walls. He was conscious of John and Bella in the shadows of the corner, and of his children wrapped in their plaids; he shivered as the wind fluttered the rags stopping up the window-pane, and, settling himself beside Allison, he closed his eyes in a vain endeavor to sleep.

She took his head upon her shoulder as the

night advanced, and he did not resist. The vision of that howling room beneath kept rising in his brain, and he saw himself driven slowly back by the gigantic figures, which shone beautifully in the lamplight.

Allison was happy: she had him for that night at least.

CHAPTER III

HAMISH woke early the following morning. The room seemed more repugnant than ever with the furtive light of dawn creeping in through the filthy window. Allison still slept, leaning uncomfortably against the chair. He thought how weary she looked, her face taking on a more childish expression than ever in sleep. For a moment compunction overwhelmed him, but he reassured himself with the thought that she would wish to be with him wherever he went; surely this fatigue would be more welcome to her than the lack of his presence? Both John and Bella in the far corners of the room snored peacefully, John with sudden short fierce grunts, Bella in a regular crescendo, which reached a certain pitch, then died away for a moment, to work up once more to its former height.

Suddenly the scene of the night before came back to him with disturbing clarity. He shuddered, and then a slow anger began to grow in his mind. He burnt with indignation at the

thought of himself standing in the passage outside the bolted door. He would show them
who was master; only give him a little time to
settle down and they should witness a great
reversal of affairs. His rage began to fade and
the spirit of pity and the spiritual elation which
saved him from being the dogmatic, purposeful
minister, common in Scotland at the time,
flooded his mind as it had the night before.
These people knew nothing, had not heard the
Word of God; he, Hamish McGregor, would
be as a voice crying in the wilderness, he would
be the one to bring the light of the Gospel into
the darkness of their ignorance. There on the
cold, silent hearth Hamish dedicated his spirit
and body to the human beings that were about
to be consigned to his charge. In one corner
of his mind lurked the sense of fear which had
been born of the storm and the flaming beauty
in the eyes of the fighting red-haired giant, but
he swept it aside.

He roused Allison gently. She opened her
great red-brown eyes, and gazed at him with an
unseeing bewilderment. He was standing
above her buttoning on his cape and smoothing
his thick brown hair.

"Wake up, my dear," he reiterated softly,

but persistently; "we must press on to Glenlee,
even though we must travel on the Sabbath.
This is no fit house for Christian folk. Rouse
yourself, Allison," he continued more irritably,
as she continued to sit gazing upward at him
with a growing weariness.

"But, Hamish," she faltered, "are we not to
get our breakfast, are we to have nothing to
eat? The children . . ." she murmured; then,
shamed by the fire of scorn in his gray eyes, she
was silent. The spirit of courage, the sense
of set determination which carried Hamish
through life like a challenge, had borne away
on its headlong course all sense of physical need.
He had not fed adequately since noon of the
previous day—the evening repast had consisted
of a few crumbled oatcakes and some scones;
but, glorying in a physical strength which put
him beyond the touch of ordinary human needs,
he had dwelt upon the future triumph of his
determination, and not upon his present bodily
sensations.

"Surely it is of more importance that the
children should leave this place, before the
drunken and unclean revelers resume consciousness?" he said with a curl of his beautifully shaped mouth. "If you could have seen

the indecent debauchery which I witnessed last night—the disgusting depths to which human nature can fall—the animal depths—" the vision of the gleaming shoulder through the torn shirt of the straining giant troubled his mind. "Would you have the children fed bodily rather than spiritually?"

Allison dropped her eyes, ashamed of what she had said, and yet—and yet perhaps there would be no spirit to prepare for an after life if the poor little bodies were starved with cold and hunger. Perhaps it did not matter—the sooner they left this life of tribulation, the better—at least so she had read in the Scriptures and Hamish had told her that in Heaven only would they obtain the peace that passeth all understanding. It had crossed her mind once or twice that Hamish, in a world where there was to be no more strife and nothing but an eternally protracted peace, would be nothing but an irritable fish out of water. She had been surprised at herself for doubting what he had expounded to her so often. In Heaven there was to be no more weeping or sadness, but by implying that Hamish would be a fish out of water, she was implying that there would at least be discontent. But then, of course, she

had reassured herself, it would no longer be
Hamish, not the Hamish that she knew, but a
new and Angelic spirit. It worried her a little
that Hamish would be no longer the real
Hamish, or perhaps the Hamish that she knew
was the unreal Hamish—at this point she would
hastily shut her mind to further possibilities
of the subject. It was all incomprehensible to
her, and nothing seemed to fit very well.

Hamish's voice broke the silence, impatiently, urging her to hurry. A moment later
he disappeared through the doorway with John,
in order to harness Paddy to the gig once more.

Allison rose stiffly to her feet and dragged
herself wearily to the corner, where Bella was
wrapping the two children in their plaids.
With anxious hands she drew the protecting
homespun round the small shoulders. Jean's
solemn gray eyes regarded her mother curiously, but a veiled anxiety no doubt lurked at
the bottom of her baby mind, an uncomfortable
feeling that her cosmos was being disarranged,
something was being omitted. She made a few
tentative inquiries as to her probable further
movements, and finally allowed an expression
of resignation to settle on her rounded features.

"Coming for a nice drive now with Mama,"

premised Allison ingratiatingly, stroking her daughter's short fluffy hair gently. It had been a shock to Allison when she had suddenly discovered that her children must call her "Mama"; she had been "Allison" to so many people for so many years (she was the youngest of four sisters) that it seemed strange that the life which she had formed from her own vitality should regard her as "Mama." However, she had become accustomed to Jean's piped "Mama," just as she had become accustomed to the reverential "Mistress McGregor," and the added aside, "the Minister's wife."

"I think we had better carry them downstairs, Bella," remarked Allison in a matter-of-fact voice; "then we shall be ready and we shan't keep the Minister waiting. I—I—" Her voice faltered, but she went on bravely, "I expect we shall be able to get some breakfast for them on the way, and it's a beautiful day after the storm. You'll enjoy the nice shiny snow," she added softly, addressing the top of her daughter's fluffy head.

Bella made no comment; she sniffed loudly, however, and rose to her feet with Alex in her arms. Allison regarded her with growing apprehension. Bella's "tantrums" were not to be ignored. One awful day she had cooked nothing for supper but a dish of potatoes, which she had planted firmly on the table before Hamish, and without a word she had stalked away with a subdued sniff. Hamish had rated her severely for this, but he had been unable to obtain any response from the restrained but purposeful Bella.

"Oh, Bella," sighed Allison, "please, please don't mind about the breakfast. I know the Minister will stop at the first respectable house. You see, we couldn't possibly stay here—we—we—mustn't feed our bodies and—and—not our spirits." Was that what Hamish had said, or had she got it all muddled?

Bella paused a moment in her stately and ponderous passage towards the door.

"Havers," she remarked quietly, but decidedly.

Allison turned away. She felt that she could not bear any more. All she wanted was to be left quiet; she was so tired, and her eyes felt like hot smoldering coals; she felt very sick, too, and her limbs were heavy as lead, yet at the same time light as air. She bowed her head and the hot weary tears welled into her eyes and crept drearily down her cheeks.

Suddenly she felt a firm touch on her shoulder, and passing her small hand quietly across her eyes she turned and gazed straight into Bella's rugged face.

The elder woman was of the unbending type of lowland Scot and forged her way through life looking at things as they were, and taking things as they came. Her creed was hard and matter-of-fact. The sight of Allison's tear-stained and weary face, so childish in its roundness, and of that slight figure weighed down with its motherhood, stirred something which lies dormant in most women. She patted Allison's shoulder, and spoke to her gently.

"Never fret, Mistress McGregor," she said with a wealth of comfort in her slow quiet voice, "it's not me to add dreichness to a dreary enough state of affairs; my breakfast's nothing to me, but there are ithers that wad be the better of it—bodies and spirits—blether—" she muttered to herself.

"Dinna ye stir, ma bairnie, and I'll take the children down one by one; ye're in no fit state to carry them, more likely ye're needin' carrying yersel'," she concluded fiercely, addressing the crooked fireplace.

In a moment she had turned, swooped Alex

off the chair where he sat patiently, and was gone.

Encouraged and strengthened, Allison went down on her knees before the small Jean, and with her arms locked round the child, said suddenly, "Now, my wee, you'll be good all day, and very, very good when your Papa speaks to you." It was a sort of subconscious reaction; she felt that by letting Bella see those weary tears, and by letting her realize the need that she had of food and rest, she had somehow been guilty of disloyalty to Hamish, she had not been the "Minister's wife" that she should have been. She kissed the child slowly and softly, wrapping her more closely in the plaid. She could hear Bella panting heavily up the creaking stairs again.

They descended together, Bella bearing the child firmly on one arm. She pushed open the door of the parlor and stalked through the kitchen much as she might have stalked through an extremely noisome pig-sty. Allison followed timidly. There were two men half-lying, and half-sitting, on a wooden bench in the corner; and seated on the floor, his great back propped against the table, was the vast red-headed man whom Hamish had seen struggling the night before. His head was thrown back, revealing the thick power of his throat and neck; he had moved in his sleep and one great arm lay carelessly across the bent shoulders of the girl that leaned against his huge side. The whiteness of his arm was accentuated by the dark brown tan of his hand. The girl's head hung downwards, and the loose tendrils of her flaxen hair lay against the dark leather of his boots.

Allison hesitated for a moment, gazing at the pair in awe. She took in the whiteness of his arm and the flaxen gleam of the girl's hair with an instinctive appreciation; something in the vitality and yet perfect repose of the two figures filled her with wonder. And then suddenly she shuddered; her eyes took in the drab details of the room, the overturned chair and dead cinders on the hearth, the spilt whisky and the dim dusty light filtering feebly into the grayness of the room. All the sense of instinctive glory left her, she was terrified by the white proprietary strength of the man's arm. She stumbled towards the door and tore it open. It stuck on the flagstones, making a hideous screeching noise as she dragged it towards her. She felt as though some indefinable terror lurked in the darkness of the Inn, and it was not until she was standing outside in the clean gleam of the snow, that she could shake off that feeling of oppression.

The world had undergone a magical change. Everything was rounded and softened. The corners of the roof and the railings were gentle and evened, and where the sun caught a slope of unbroken snow, a thousand diamond facets dazzled her eyes; the branches of the lonely little tree that stood to the left of the door were mossed with a white delicacy, making a gentle network against the unbroken blue of the sky. Her feet crunched with muffled squeaks across the sloping, rounded sequence of snow. Down the glen the sun was reflected along the tops of the mountains in streaks of more dazzling whiteness. She stood lost in wonder for a moment, filled with a fear of breaking the beauty of the silence, the trancelike suspension of the world. It seemed to her an eternity as she stood there gazing, her spirit yearning—for what? Then a robin darted swiftly across her vision, settling like a dark feather on the snow-smoothed fence. The clearness of its inquiring twitter broke the stillness, and Allison started guiltily forward in the direction of the stable-yard.

The yard itself presented an animated scene in contrast to the silent impenetrability of the snow-mantled world outside. Paddy was already harnessed to the gig, whilst Hamish was giving a final tightening to the frost-hardened straps. The stamp of the other horse echoed from the stable, ringing clear through the transparent air. John's voice mumbled on a lower key, as his slow footsteps moved about the resounding stable. Bella stood with the two children in her arms, her face imperturbable, although their combined weight was no light one.

Hamish stood back, swinging his arms and blowing on his numbed fingers. His brown hair was blown about by the breeze, and a keen light shone in his gray eyes. A quick pleasure thrilled through him at the sight of the unbroken purity of the snow. He filled his lungs with the clean newborn air, shutting out the thought of the gray dusty parlor with its sleeping, depraved humanity.

"Up you get, my dear," he cried, assisting Allison to ascend into the gig; his arms were both round her and with a powerful swing he half lifted her into the seat. The bright clear light that shone in his eyes tempted her to lean forward, laying her cheek against his.

"There's room for Jean between us, Hamish," she pleaded softly. "It will be better so—the seat is too wide and shakes me from side to side!" Emboldened by his acquiescent silence, she brushed her lips gently over his forehead.

He had not heard what she had said; his eyes, with the torchlight flare of intelligence, gazed to the far peaks flanking the glen through which they must pass; their clean-cut austerity pleased his senses. He felt Allison's caress against his forehead, and drew away his eyes from the distance to let their gaze fall upon her. For a moment he was a man, not an idea or a spiritual enthusiasm given form and shape, and he loved her as one individual soul loves another. He held her gently, almost reverently, his eyes moving slowly from her brown eyes to her small gentle mouth. Nothing else existed for a moment; it was as if he had a spell cast over him . . . Paddy moved restlessly forward, pawing the snow with impatient hoof . . . the spell was broken, and with a kind of snapping jerk the minister drew his arms away; he gath-

ered the reins in his hands and prepared to
mount beside her.

"But may she?" continued Allison doubt-
fully. This strange saint-like husband of hers
was more than she could pretend to understand, with his hard image-like front, that he
suddenly exposed at least-expected moments;
you might stretch out a hand to him for comfort and feel the hot burning kisses of adora-
tion, you might feel only the cold marble of
"unassailable righteousness."

"May you what?" he answered, lifting his
head in surprise.

She faltered her request again, gazing anxiously down at him in uncertainty. With a
laugh that scattered the silence of the snow,
he snatched the small muffled Jean from Bella's
arms, and swung her up beside Allison. "Now
are you satisfied, O Mother of the World!"
he laughed. He was up beside them in a second, and urging the old pony out through the
yard gate, cheering it on as it picked its way
gingerly along the crunching snow-covered
road.

The sun was behind them, and before them
lay the clear-cut wonder of light breaking up
the deep luminous shadows on the mountains

of the narrow gorge; their minds were filled with the peace which is so magnificent, yet so pathetic, in man. What is it that makes man crave for joy, and then when he thinks he has attained it, discover that, like the summit of a mountain, it has retired from him and eluded his grasp; then as he stumbles forward again, and by chance happens to look behind, he finds that he has left the peak behind him unaware, and that he is traveling hourly further from it, and he cannot return, he cannot wait, he must always go forward?

The bright reflection thrown up from the snow lit up the two faces with an unnatural brilliance, showing them in their youthful expectancy, looking forward into a clearly defined future, silhouetted, as it were, against the cloudless blue.

Chapter IV

IT was night before the gig arrived at the summit of Ben Buie, whence the winding road creeps down into the heart of Glenlee. Darkness had fallen long ago, so thickly that the circle of lamplight from the gig was clear-cut, illuminating the snow-rutted road, but failing to penetrate the moorland by which it was flanked. Down below by the bay a few lights twinkled, and in the vast silence Allison heard the sound she was to bear in her heart as the essence of the Glenlee days, for evermore, the ceaseless sigh of the sea.

Slowly they wound their way down the slope, until they came to the sea's edge at the bottom. Hamish dismounted, and, leaving the gig, went towards one of the flickering lights in order to discover the whereabouts of the keys of the Manse. Cold, sudden little blasts came up off the sea, and as Allison sat huddled on the seat of the gig, her arms protecting the sleeping child, she was suddenly frozen by a primeval terror. How long she sat stiff and upright she did not know, her eyes open and aching, vainly attempting to penetrate the horror of the darkness. She thought she heard voices sometimes, and then the silence came surging back, and she sat once more, listening as though her eardrums would burst. Still Hamish did not come. A stone rattled down the bank onto the shore and she felt in her overtired mind as though something had moved in the darkness. She thought she saw shadows move and disappear, and yet again there was nothing but the silence and immensity of the darkness and the sighing of the sea.

Hamish came back, his heavy tread friendly in the distance. He climbed up beside her and whipped up the pony, his jaw thrust out in anger.

"Where must we go now?" queried Allison, and, "Oh, Hamish, did you—" She hesitated. "The place is so lonely and yet there are so many people—it lives and yet it is dead."

He looked at her sharply, but vouchsafed no answer.

Presently he turned the gig in through the moss-covered gate-posts of the Manse, which was situated half a mile up the hill. The wheels rattled over the drive, which was thinly covered with snow owing to the thick canopy of trees which clung together forming a roof over it.

Hamish pulled up opposite the door, and drawing a key from beneath his cloak, descended and unlocked the door. He lifted Allison and Jean down and, half carrying them, half leading them, he drew them into the darkness inside the house. A smell of must and stale air greeted their nostrils. Allison clung to Hamish's arm in the darkness.

"I must go and stable Paddy," he said slowly, as if thinking of something else. "They would not come with me from the cottage, Allison; they would hardly give me the key, they would spare nothing for us to eat—I told them of the bairns and still they kept on saying, 'We have no food,' and these—these are to be my people—God's people."

The weariness in his voice was like a reviving spirit to Allison. She let him disengage himself and she cowered alone with Jean in the dark hall, her heart thudding as though it were leaping up and down in her breast. She could hear the slight movement of paper in the corner as though rats were scampering over old, long-disused scraps of rubbish.

Presently Hamish returned, carrying a gig-

lamp in either hand. He carefully closed the
door and shot the screaming reluctant bolts.
Holding the lamps above his head he surveyed
the hall. The dust lay thick everywhere;
scraps of paper and broken pottery littered the
floor. A couple of rats scuttered away into the
darkness beneath the stairs. On the right a
door stood open. Slowly he crossed the hall
and disappeared through it into the room beyond.

The scene was dancing before Allison's travel-
wearied eyes; she swayed and voices surged in
her ears, and the rush of water. She sank to
her knees with a quiet lost little cry, still clutching the child by the hand. But Hamish had
heard, and came hurrying back. In a moment
he was beside her and the sobbing child, he was
chafing her hands, smoothing her hair, speaking
in a low tone, the beautiful fulness of his voice
lingering over the words of the most caressive
language in the world—the Gaelic. She clung
to him terrified at first, and then by degrees a
peace descended on her and she slept, covered
with his cloak.

Later John and Bella came in, and in a half-
sleep Allison saw her other baby, and with a
warm satisfaction she fell asleep once more.

Hamish lay awake longer. His mind was red-hot with weariness, the unwilling, almost evil faces of the men in the tumbled down cottage he had visited, tormented his vision. The continuous drip of the thawing snow from the eaves drove him nearly to madness. Presently he dozed; he woke once again with a start, the vision of the red-headed giant of the Neabost Inn vivid before his eyes; and then he slept.

The dawn broke in streaks of pale fire over a world where the thaw had set in—great blobs of melted snow slid from branch to branch. The water dripped steadily from a sodden thatch of the crofts down by the sea.

Allison woke stiff and cold, to find that Hamish had already risen, and was carrying peats in a basket from which the water dripped in a melancholy stream. He left a trail of melted snow and mud across the dusty floor of the hall.

The dirt and squalor of the place was very apparent in the daylight; the paper hung drunkenly forward from the wall as if listening; in one corner the livid dampness had eaten through the ceiling. Somewhere through the door beneath the stairs, she could hear the sound of Bella's voice and the clatter of dishes; the good soul was engaged already in unpacking the few belongings that had been brought in the cart.

Allison stretched her arms upward, then she rose on her toes; she stood for a moment yawning widely. A pale watery shaft of sunlight faltered through the front door, which stood ajar. She went out, lifting her head to breathe the freshness of the morning air. She turned and regarded her home for the first time. Later on it seemed incredible to her that there should ever have been a time when the little square house had not been welded into her very being; it seemed as though she must have been born with the knowledge of it, and of its expectant watchful atmosphere.

The house was square, built of solid gray stone; two chimney-stacks stood up, one at either side of the roof, like hard, prick ears; there were three windows facing the front on the first floor, at that time blank and mysterious, like unseeing eyes. On the ground floor the square front door, from which the paint was peeling in thin ribbons, was flanked by a window on either side. Trees grew right over the house behind; great branches stretched with greedy, dripping fingers along the roof. In

front there was a small clearing, through which
the house peered at the distant hills of the
Islands. Piles of dead leaves, sodden to a rich
umber color, lay heaped where the wind had
blown them into banks against the house and
along the sides of the drive.

Everything was absolutely silent, save for the
continuous dripping of the melted snow and
the sudden isolated twitter of a robin; so silent
that Allison started nervously at the shuffle of a
patch of snow as it dislodged itself from the
sloping roof and thundered to the ground. To
the left of the house towered the rock-strewn
side of Ben Buie, patched here and there with
stretches of snow; higher up lay slopes of a
dazzling whiteness which melted into a swirl of
mist that dipped and moved like some living
thing. A burn, brown against the purity of the
snow, hurled its way downward among the
rocks.

Up there all seemed pulsating with a mysterious hurried life, but down in the glen where
she stood, the damp immobility was almost op-
pressive. She entered the house once more,
rubbing her hands together for warmth.

In the kitchen all was confusion. A fire
burned briskly in the rusted grate, over which a

kettle hung, suspended from an iron hook and chain. Bella was almost totally immersed in a wooden packing-case, from which she was extracting pots and pans, oatmeal, clothing, knives, bedding, string, nails and all manner of oddments. These lay strewn about the dusty floor. Alex was jabbering softly to himself. He was occupying another empty packing-case and was enveloped in a huge tartan plaid. Jean hurried delightedly about the dusty floor, examining everything she found with bright inquisitive eyes, her little face smeared with dust, her bright fluffy hair decorated with scraps of plaster. She kept up an unending flow of conversation.

Bella rushed from the packing-case to the fireplace, gave a furious stir to a pan of porridge which stood there, and then bolted head-first into the packing-case once more. She kept up a running flow of conversation in a muttered undertone. She admonished Jean and uttered threats of a devastating nature against those who had left the house in such a state of uncleanliness.

Hamish had disappeared down to the sea's edge. His furniture should have arrived long since; he had despatched it by water several

days before he had set out on his journey. The
natives of Glenlee were taciturn and suspicious
—no sail had been sighted, but then the weather
had been very bad, very bad indeed; no boat
would be venturing into the bay at all at all,
with the wind in the southwest. But surely
now, Hamish thought, now that the wind had
dropped and the sea lay before him calm and
undisturbed, little tongues of dark water lick-
ing at the round gray boulders at his feet,
the boat would come. He beat his freezing
fingers against his side so that they tingled with
pain. Across the sound the mountains of the
Islands stood clear-cut, decorated with the snow.
The silence sank into his being as it had into
that of Allison. He seemed as though he could
not move, but must stand there gazing forever.

Suddenly, round the southern headland appeared a boat, tacking and veering in the morning light. The wind was rising now and a stiff
breeze tossed the little ship hither and thither
as it rounded the point. Hamish turned, delighted. Here was his furniture, after all—
everything would be all right; he had, in fact,
arranged things as they should be. He would
stroll back to the Manse and inform Allison
that she might prepare the rooms for the furni-

ture, which was waiting ready to take its place in its new home. As he hurried up the hill towards the gate, he saw himself seated in his own green leather chair, with a fire burning in the grate and his books arranged neatly round him in their shelves, and the tobacco jar on the mantelpiece, the one that had always stood on the mantelpieces that had accompanied the different stages of his life, a jar in the form of a dolphin's head with wide open jaws and delicately frilled gills. He had bought it years ago in his student days in Glasgow; he had seen it in the middle of the tobacconist's window and known at once that it must be his. It was these familiar possessions that he needed near him, the tobacco jar, and Allison sewing opposite to him. Once he could stretch out his hand and feel these friendly presences about him, he would fear no longer the intangible "something" which haunted him.

Breakfast was spread on one of the packing-cases in the kitchen. Curls of steam rose from the bowls of porridge, and the firelight glinted on the great mugs of milk which Bella had produced from nowhere, much as a conjuror produces a white rabbit from some part of his mysterious person.

Hamish was elated; the fresh wintry air seemed to emanate from his person, he "over-flowed" the little gathering, slapping his lips over the porridge, pouring the milk down his throat as though he had no swallowing apparatus whatsoever. He seemed too enormous for the dingy room.

Allison watched him with admiration. She was tired and dejected; she had smiled at his triumph as he had poured the news of the furniture's arrival into her ears. He was pleased and proud, and quite rightly, so she thought. Here was the furniture, the very furniture which was part of her old life and her first home; it lay waiting to take up its place in the new Manse. Perhaps "waiting to take up its place" was not the right phrase; it could not take up its own place—that was the trouble. It had to have the place made for it. A weight of despair descended upon her; she glanced at the damp mildewed walls, the hanging paper—yes, that was the trouble, a place must be made for it; and, then, there were only three pairs of curtains—what was to be done about a pair for the hall? And she was sure that the table would be too big for the small dining-room, and probably all the blankets would be damp and—her brain

trembled under the tediousness of her thought;
all this worry was like a dull heavy object at
the bottom of her mind, which was always
there, do what you would.

As soon as he had swallowed his breakfast,
Hamish was gone, hurrying down the road to
the cluster of crofts by the sea. The boat was
opposite now, but was continuing its course
towards the northern headland. The wind had
risen to a hurricane; no doubt the landing was
impossible. A kind of despair seized him; he
must have his furniture and his coal (of which
there was a small quantity on board the vessel).
Always these elemental forces seemed to come
between him and his desires—first the snow and
now the wind. He watched the ship disappear
behind the headland, then he turned and retraced his steps towards the crofts. Peering
through the dark square of the doorway of the
first one, he greeted the house in his soft Gaelic.
Inside it was dark save for the faint light from
the tiny window, and the glow from the open
peat fire. In the corner he could discern dimly
the outline of the square bed let into the wall.
A figure was bending over the peats; it raised
its head at the sound of Hamish's voice. A face
looked at him out of the darkness, a face as old

and irresistible as the mountains, and the wind and the sea.

"Are any of the men about, good wife?" he inquired slowly. "I would beg of them to help me with their boats—my gear is on board the vessel which has put in round the far headland, feared to wait in the bay because of the wind. I must fetch the things by boat and land them myself."

She gazed at him mournfully, shaking her old head slowly to and fro. "The wind is too strong," was all she said, in a voice that was at one with the darkness and solitude of the cottage.

He persisted in his inquiry, however, and presently she hobbled to the doorway and pointed with a finger to the shore, where figures could be seen struggling with their ungainly brown fishing-nets in the wind.

Hamish hurried towards them. There were six or seven men, more Saxon in appearance than Celtic, tall spare men with a quiet ruminative gaze. Hamish stated his desire, throwing out his hands in his eagerness, and turning to them one after another. But they would not move, they shook their heads. The same withdrawal seemed to take place that had taken place the night before when he had asked them for food and for the key of the Manse.

He felt alone again, an isolated figure in a world of tumult. All the exhilaration of the morning had gone. Then suddenly the spirit entered him which was like the plunging of clean hard steel into his mind, the spirit that had filled him with a joy as he had battled through the snow on his way back from the Neabost Inn to find Bella and the children. He was more than these men, more than these warring elements; he knew the Divine Spirit that was in him. Fierce scorn rang in his tone as he made one last appeal.

"Is there no man will come with me, no man that does not fear a puff of wind?"

Still they did not move. He turned away, leaving them standing motionless like a carved fresco. And then one of them stepped forward slowly and quietly.

"My boat is lying below the Minnoch Creek," he said gently. "I will come with you for your gear."

Hamish turned. A young man stood before him, short and dark, his face burned to a deep brown, his eyes direct and shining like blue glass. Here was the true Celt. The hostility was not there, that veiled enmity which puzzled Hamish so much.

Together they approached the creek and set out silently across the dancing stretch of water. All day they toiled with the small boat, round the northern headland and into the bay, bringing now a couple of chairs and a table, now a load of coal. John met them on the shore and labored backwards and forwards with the cart. As they brought the last load, the night had almost closed in. The arch of the sky was a dark translucent blue, cut with a tiny embroidery of stars. The wind had abated and the breath of the two men steamed in the frosted air.

"I must thank you, Donald," said Hamish slowly. "We have done a good day's work— we have done what we set out to do." And indeed they had. Hamish's hands were sore with shoveling coal and clinging onto the frozen sheets, and his back was stiff with the weights he had lifted.

"Tell me," he asked suddenly, as they climbed up from the shore towards the lights of the crofts, "why would the others not come?" He had seen the men standing about all day, mending their nets or leaning against their door-posts dreaming.

But Donald would not answer. As they came level with the crofts Hamish stretched out his work-scarred hand. "Good night and you have my gratitude." The young fisherman took it slowly. "Good night to you," he replied simply, and then suddenly in an undertone, "They're feared and they hate what they canna rightly understand, that's why they would na give you a loan of their boats."

"Feared?" questioned Hamish; but Donald had gone, swallowed in the darkness.

That night Hamish sat by a fire in his favorite green leather chair, and his eyes rested peacefully on the dolphin tobacco jar. His was the only room that Bella and Allison had managed to bring to a semblance of order. White and worn out, Allison sat opposite to him after a day of dust, sharp packing-cases, and of endless running up and down of stairs. Her eyes were almost closed in sleep, but Hamish did not notice, his shone, and he gazed beyond her in a kind of ecstasy.

"They are feared and—they hate what they canna understand," he repeated slowly, almost to himself, "but the spirit of man triumphs over adversity, they cannot stop me. I sit here in my own study with all my own possessions around me." He glanced fondly at the tobacco jar and the piles of unsorted books. "I will teach them to understand. I alone—through the spirit of the Lord—have triumphed."

Allison's tired eyes filled with tears; she bent lower over her knitting—he alone—well, of course, if he had not rescued the furniture there could have been no study, but the memory of the bitter coldness of her fingers as she drew book after book from the packing-cases, filled her mind. Then she was ashamed, and raising her eyes, full of tears as they were (for he would never notice to-night, not with that far light shining in his face), she said softly:

"Won't you read to me, Hamish?"

"Why, of course, my dear. What shall I read?"

She rose silently and brought his worn volume of Cowper to him. He turned the pages idly. "What shall I read, Allison?" he said again absently.

"Will you read 'The Poplar Field'?" she asked softly, turning over the pages to find the place. He took the book from her absently and began to read in his full beautiful voice; a sadness crept into his tone as he read the last two verses:

"My fugitive years are all hasting away,
  And I must ere long lie as lowly as they
With a turf on my breast and a stone at my head,
Ere another such grove shall arise in its stead.

'Tis a sight to engage me, if anything can,
To muse on the perishing pleasures of man,
Though his life be a dream, his enjoyments I see
Have a being less durable even than he."

There was a silence in the room for a moment.

"No, Allison," Hamish said suddenly, "I won't read Cowper to you any more." He stretched out his hand for his Bible, and began almost immediately in a voice of suppressed emotion, the Fifty-ninth Psalm.

" 'Deliver me from mine enemies, O God: defend me from those that rise up against me.— Stand up, O Lord God of Hosts, thou God of Israel to visit all the heathen: and be not merciful unto them that offend of malicious wickedness.—My strength will I ascribe unto Thee, for Thou art the God of my refuge.— Unto Thee, O my strength, will I sing, for Thou, O God, art my refuge and my merciful God."

A tear trickled down Allison's cheek. Something seemed to be finished for her; a door was closing behind her which could never be opened again, she must always go on and on, fearfully pushing open other doors, not knowing what lay beyond them. Hamish seemed to be singing a hymn of praise to his own strength; she felt crushed and apprehensive at his overwhelming self-confidence.

Chapter V

THE actual village of Glenlee was situated almost at the sea's edge, where the waters of the river hurried in a gleaming amber mass towards the bay. It was composed of a few crofts, flanking the grass-grown road, most of them stone with blunted corners and roughly thatched roofs; a few turf huts remained, however, which had survived the ages. The bay itself was open to the roaring southwest gales that drove up the sound from the Atlantic; in bad weather no ships could linger in the bay while boats rowed out to them. There was no landing-stage. Farther north the tides were treacherous and the water swirled and roared, especially when the tide and wind were in opposite directions. The shore shelved down rapidly in great rounded mounds of pebbles. The road ran along the sea's edge for a short distance (where stood the bleak little church) and then climbed steeply over the northern headland, dwindling as it went into a mere track. It plunged over the summit and crept down towards the dark cloud-smoking waters of Loch Doul, where it lost itself forever in the mighty cloud-capped mountains at the head of the loch.

The Manse stood up the glen a good half-mile from the sea's edge. The road wound slowly upwards, the steeps of Scurr Dubh on the right and Ben Buie jutting angrily into the heavens on the left. Great trees grew round the Manse, planted at some earlier date, and looking strange among those naked hills. They were mighty trees, however, sycamores, ashes, beeches, firs, even a Spanish chestnut grew here and there. The lonely square-faced little house looked down the glen to the sea and the dark mountains of Isle Sora. Behind it the hills seemed to close in where the road wound upwards over narrow little bridges towards Loch Dreich.

The farm was attached behind the Manse and the sheep wandered over six hundred acres of hill and moorland in the upper glen. The whitewashed buildings were surrounded with sturdy hedges of beech and fuchsia. Often the clouds were so low that they almost seemed to touch the house itself and rest on the bosom of the sea below.

The loneliness and the silence of the glen filled Allison with a nameless fear, and yet the silence was ever filled with sound, indescribable sound, the quintessence of wind and rushing water and the rhythm of the sea beating forever on the shore. Sight and hearing seemed to her to be obscured: the sublime mystery of the shrouded mountains, the muffled beat of the waters, seemed to come to her through the soft veil of the mist.

As she sat in the square parlor of the Manse, idly knitting garments for the child which was to come, her eyes wandered restlessly round the room. The Manse was in order now, although the damp still ran down the walls in livid streaks and dripped through the ceilings of the upper rooms. Still the branches of the trees behind the house tapped furtively on the windows and the moss-covered slates.

It was a month since that snowy night when she had slept in Hamish's arms in the draughty hall, the rats and the wind scuttering about amongst the torn paper. She had hardly seen Hamish since then except when he lay asleep beside her. She loved him with a love which was tinged with melancholy because something told her that a far-away horn had blown, al-

though she had failed to hear it; the echo filled
her with listlessness and dread.

Hamish toiled from morning till night. He
had discovered that there was no Kirk Session,
and thus no Elders. There was no Poor Fund
and the Sacrament had not been administered
for over two years. Worst of all, in the dark
crofts that he entered, the Word of God was
unknown. Coming from a well-ordered parish,
a hundred miles farther south, Hamish was appalled and dismayed at the ignorance of the
people, people who did not even possess a Bible.
No man here, in his opinion, was worthy of the
position of Elder. Anger stirred in him; he
challenged their shifty eyes with his own pierc-
ing directness of gaze, he scorned their soft
docility that made them shake their heads and
say in their slow careful voices that it was "many
years indeed" since they had had a Bible of
their own. When he spoke of the Sacrament
they shook their heads mournfully. Then, in
the midst of his anger and scorn, that overwhelming sense of pity would envelop him; yet
he was afraid of their quiet indifference and of
a hidden power which lurked behind their
dreaming eyes.

From morning till night he worked, organizing his parish, ministering to the poor from his own slender pocket, visiting the sick, presenting the crofters with crude cheap Bibles from the Bible Society; and now, as the month drew to a close, he had sent round the tokens for the Sacrament to the few whom he deemed worthy. Many of these he had had to deliver himself, riding upon Paddy over miles of trackless moorland to visit the outskirts of his widespread parish, and no man's hand was lifted to aid him.

The administrations of the Sacrament and the preachings attached were to last four and a half days, and the crofters from the outlying farms were to be housed in the great barn which lay at the back of the Manse. Sacks of meal were to be provided for them and milk from Hamish's own cows. He had only one other minister to assist with the preaching.

Deep in his heart Hamish had feared that the people would not come, that the hostility which he saw in their glance would keep them away, but on the Thursday morning, as the gray light began to brighten over the wind-tossed sea, boats were seen in the bay and figures appeared on the road that twisted its way into the glen. Little black dots of humanity moved slowly along with an occasional cart and horse. Slowly they wound their way towards the gray kirk which stood on a rise above the sea.

Hamish preached to them like a man possessed, choosing a green place on the glebeland above the church for the pitching of his tent. The wind tore round the corner of the rocks in sudden fits of anger and the trees at the southwest end lashed themselves into a fury, like mocking elusive spirits.

On the Friday night the people slept quietly in the barn, the women huddled together at one end, and the men at the other. The Saturday dawned on a rain-soaked dismal world, and still the black figures moved slowly down the ribbon of road, like flies on some patterned cloth.

The wind was like a ragged-edged knife, torturing the men in their black suits and scattering the women, who stood in suffering clumps, to the shelter of the trees.

Allison, knitting in the Manse parlor, could catch a glimpse of the road through the side window. All morning it had rained; drenched black figures had moved across her vision like an automatic sequence of midgets. It was noon now and the wind had risen to the full glory of its strength, the rain shattered against the window in sudden startling showers. As she raised her eyes to the window, at the sound of footsteps on the road, she saw a figure pass which roused her curiosity. The man was clad in ragged clothes, and he wore a battered green bonnet at a jaunty angle. He was wheeling a small gaily painted handcart.

Allison rose and crossed to the window in order to see more of this strange newcomer. She pulled the curtains aside, and even went as far as to open the window a little (for Hamish had made all the Manse windows to open), but the hungry wind rushed into the room, swaying the pictures and causing the fire to puff out disgusted clouds of blue smoke. She shuddered with cold and desolation, and closed the window again quickly. The rain seemed to have soaked into her mind, and it seemed to her that she would hear eternally the varied music of water, water rushing in torrents down the steep side of Ben Buie, water pattering furtively in raindrops outside the window, water surging rhythmically in the waves of the sea, and lastly, water creeping and oozing stealthily down the walls and through the ceilings of the rooms.

Spring and the dry yellow light of summer seemed something incredible, a dream or a

memory. Even the white hard beauty of the
snow seemed to be a mere fantasy of the brain.
She thought of the day—a month ago, it seemed
now an age past and dead—when she had stood
outside the Neabost Inn, drinking in the silence
and power of the snow-clad world; a spirit had
stirred within her that had made her yearn for
an indescribable glory with which to fill her
life; the earth about her had seemed laid forth
as though to receive a bride, it paid homage to
her as its most perfect creation. But now she
was a lonely frightened soul, standing on some
colossal threshold which she dare not cross, the
earth and the elements surged around her, bat-
tering her to and fro, mocking and laughing
at her midget-like ineffectuality.

Perhaps she would never see the pale shadow
of green brighten over the branches of winter,
or wake to hear the expectant voice of the birds,
or see the seagulls floating over the sea as though
time stood still for them. A fear haunted her.
She had lived through the birth of two children; would she live through the birth of the
third? An unreasoning terror crept into her
mind. She would die and they would bury her
in that rain-soaked earth in the churchyard
above the sea, the waves would lash the very

walls of the graveyard on stormy days, and she would be below the sodden ground and would hear the far-away echo of the waters. She was angry when she allowed these thoughts to take possession of her mind. She would persuade herself over and over again that death was a sleep from which one awoke, to find oneself restored and at one with the Spirit from which life had been drawn. But again and again crept back the idea of her own individual soul; dead or alive, surely it would be she, Allison, that would pass through the realms of death to emerge on the other side into a new life; and then the disturbing torture of the thought that no one knew anything of this mystery would gnaw at her mind. There was some brink over which the shuddering, terrified human soul disappeared, and no one—no one in the whole world—ever returned. Nevermore did one "live" or see the world about one, or touch the people that one loved—meantime the body lay in the cold clay of the sea-girt churchyard. "The body is nothing," she would repeat, "when the spirit is flown." She would glance at her own hands clasped in her lap and shudder; the body is nothing, yet it was *her* body, part of herself, and always she saw the wet earth clinging to her own hands.

It was only on particularly dreamy dark afternoons that Allison allowed these nervous fancies to torment her brain, afternoons when Hamish was absent, and she had no need to keep up an appearance, or to hurry to and fro in search of occupation. She fought against this neurasthenia bravely, and sometimes a glory filled her when she thought of the life within her—when she ruminated on the power of creation which lay with her—she clung to this elation as a stronghold in the black seething mass of uncertainty; the power of creation was hers, and nothing could riddle the knowledge with wormholes of doubt.

It was no good attempting to gather comfort from Hamish. In his presence she felt ashamed of the doubts and fears which haunted her. She tried eagerly to believe with him, and sometimes when she was with him the white flame of his faith would penetrate into her mind; but, left alone, the doubts and fears would come crawling from the hiding-places to which she had banished them. Besides, it was so seldom now that there was a moment of leisure in which she could speak to her husband. He seemed to

be far away from her, and yet she felt sure that
the Hamish she knew, the Hamish who would
read Cowper and Milton and even Herrick to
her, and who would hold her hand in his, ador-
ing her, was there behind his familiar outward
semblance. Yet she felt as though she would
be trespassing if she were to enter the garden
of his mind which she had shared with him for
six years; the thoughts which grew there, and
which she knew so well, seemed to be prohib-
ited. She felt she must avert her eyes; in fact,
she must never think of their wanderings together in the garden, because perhaps it was
by mistake that he had opened the gate to her.
It seemed to her that he had shut away that
particular garden, and passed on to another,
into which she could not enter. This new garden was lighted by the persistent gleam of his
faith; in it grew unfamiliar plants on which he
lavished his energy.

Often, as he sat thinking on the opposite side
of the fireplace in his study, she would look at
him strangely, and mourn secretly that she
could no longer anticipate the observation
which would be the outcome of his speculation.
She could no longer follow his thoughts: they
flitted from the trivialities of the Poor Fund and

the manipulation of the Kirk Session, to the overwhelming desire in him to conquer in the name of the Spirit in which he believed. It seemed to her as though he moved steadily onward, and that she could not keep pace.

As darkness drew in over the short dreary afternoon, Allison heard the sound of many footsteps mounting the hill road, and tramping over the stones of the yard on their way to the barn where shelter and warmth awaited them. The footsteps seemed to her strangely light, and the sound of voices calling cheerfully to one another above the sound of the wind came to her ears. Once she thought she heard a strong male voice singing, but before she could be certain, the wind had torn the sound away. A feeling of uneasiness began to assail her. On the other evenings the people's steps had dragged wearily across the cobbles of the yard, and they had gathered quietly round the open fire inside the barn, reading the cheap new Bibles that Hamish had given them, or conversing with one another on religious subjects in low voices.

The sound of voices grew louder, snatches of laughter swelled and dwindled on the wind.

Presently Bella entered with the lamp. Her face was square and grim in the shadow; she said nothing except, "Why, Mistress McGregor, you should have cried on me before, wearing out your puir eyes wi' straining at the bairn's tatting." She placed the lamp on the table and turned to go, but as she did so, the noise from the barn, which had risen in force since the door into the hall had been opened, reached its climax.

The wail of bagpipes rose above the storm, and almost instantaneously the stamp of excited feet could be heard.

Speechless, the two women stared at each other. At last Allison rose slowly, saying quietly, "What is it, Bella?"

The older woman cast down her eyes, shaking her head forlornly.

"Tell me what it is," insisted Allison. "Don't you see," she continued eagerly, "it must be stopped at once—at once, do you hear —the Minister will be in any moment now."

But Bella, usually so glib with her tongue, was silent.

"Very well," continued Allison quietly after a short pause, "I must go and see for myself," and she walked towards the door.

Bella laid a hand on her arm and said quickly in low tones in which pity and shame mingled, "Dinna trouble yersel', Mistress McGregor, it is the drink that is in them; it will be neither God nor man that will stop their debauching this night."

Allison stopped dead. "The drink?" she repeated in a dazed fashion, drawing her hand across her forehead as though she were wiping something away. "But, Bella, they have been down since the forenoon, down at the Sacrament."

Bella smiled grimly, but she shook her head. "It is the man in the Highland bonnet," she said slowly. "John was telling me that he set up his wares in the trees ayont the kirkyard."

Tnen she understood—the pedler with the gaily painted handcart that she had seen early in the day—he it was that was responsible for the skirl of the pipes, the stamp of feet and the high-pitched voices that reached her. A blind fury took hold of her at the thought that this man should have dared to erect his loathly stall beside the holy ground where Hamish stood, exhausted and elated, preaching to the people, straining to instil into them the spirit of purity and greatness. Anger rose in her against the people, despicable objects for whom he had worked, toiling night and day, and this was their response. Light shone in her soft brown eyes, and with a set face she walked slowly towards the kitchen.

"Ye canna go!" pleaded Bella, detaining her by the arm. "They'll maybe do you some hurt! Wait till the Minister comes in to his supper—think of the bairn that's to come so soon!"

But Allison's mind was made up. She could not bear the thought of Hamish, wounded by these wild, beastlike creatures. She cared little for their "sacrilege," but protect Hamish she would, come what might; she could imagine his tortured face as he returned exhausted from his third day's preaching.

Allison opened the back door which led into the yard. The wind rushed past her and damp brown leaves rustled into the kitchen; the rain made silver streaks across the dark square framed in the doorway, as the lamplight caught it.

The noise surged towards her, and through the doorway of the barn she could see rapidly moving figures, on which the red of the firelight was reflected. The wind almost took her breath away as she struggled across the uneven cobbles which gleamed in the shaft of lamp-

light thrown out from the kitchen door.
Above her head the branches creaked and
groaned, clawing fruitlessly at the slates of the
roof.

She pushed her way breathlessly through the
open door of the barn and stood for a moment
to recover herself. Bella stood in the doorway
behind her, a ludicrous figure, the wind tearing at her wisps of gray hair, and swirling her
apron about her in white billows.

The barn of the Glenlee Manse was of large
dimensions. The rafters were almost black
with age and smoke, the floor was strewn with
chaff; in the middle was a large sunk fireplace
lined with scorched bricks. Through the wide
chinks in the far wall the noses of the cows
were thrust, their monotonous jaws moving
slowly, strings of saliva trailing from their
gleaming lips. The smell of cows and hay per-
vaded the atmosphere, which was thickened by
the smoke from the peat fire. In the center of
the floor, strutting to and fro, was the pedler;
his brightly painted handcart stood beside him
and beneath his arm he held his pipes; for the
moment he had ceased playing.

Men and women were grouped around the
fire; the wind moved their hair and the glow

of the fire lit up their faces, giving them a fantastic appearance.

For a moment Allison was spellbound. A man and a woman close to where she stood were locked in an embrace. She saw the woman's head fall back and the gleam of the fire on her throat; she saw, too, the hunger and rapture on the man's face. Fear began to creep into her mind; her eyes passed rapidly round the ring of faces. The furtive hostile look was gone, the eyes of the people shone; they laughed and moved, at one with the wind. Allison was afraid to break the spell. Then a man staggered and fell drunkenly forward, spilling the whisky from a mug which he held. In a moment the disgust and rage surged back into her soul, and she shuddered at the sordidness of the scene.

Her voice rose shrill and fierce. The people turned and beheld in the doorway a small white-faced figure. They were silent for a moment, and then they turned away from her and took no more notice. The pedler raised the mouthpiece of his pipes and the discordant groan of the drones rent the air. Tears sparkled in Allison's eyes. She fought her way through the crowd to the center of the room. She raised her hand to strike the mouthpiece away from the pedler's lips; but suddenly a silence fell upon the people and her agonized, "Stop! Stop!" rang through a perfect stillness in the barn.

She looked up. There in the doorway stood Hamish, returned an hour before he was expected. His thick brown hair was blown back from his brow, and his face shone in the glare of the fire, the flames of which suddenly leapt up greedily, casting gigantic shapes of wavering light over the barn.

He wore no cape, and even in that tense moment Allison found herself thinking of the dampness of his clothes.

He made his way silently among the people until he stood by her side. He took her arm and led her towards the door, where Bella waited, and all the time there was no sound from the people. Then quite suddenly a woman gave a short hysterical laugh and the spell which seemed to bind them was broken. They began to move again and to whisper among themselves.

Hamish bent down and said slowly in a voice from which all feeling was absent, "Go in with

Bella, Allison; it is cold for you out here in the barn."

She whispered eagerly, "Let me stay by you, Hamish." His eyes, looking into hers, were like the eyes of a blind man, dazed and dull. The weariness in his face tore her with a desperate ineffective pity. It was then that the woman's hysterical laugh broke the silence. Still with his arm through hers, Hamish turned and faced them. It gave him control to feel Allison's trembling arm through his. His voice rang out in its full richness.

"You can go now," he said almost wearily. "You can go out into the rain and the wind. I have housed you and fed you; you have received the Spirit of the Lord—and this is the result. Not men, but animals—scarcely animals, but a pollution of the earth—you stand there as a desecration of whatever purity there is in the world. Evilness will be consumed forever in the flames." His voice rose and trembled with anger at the end. Then he began again slowly: "The women may rest here the night, but with the morning they must be gone." He turned on his heel and went into the wind-swept courtyard.

No sound had interrupted him as he spoke.

Like children the men gathered together their belongings. Then the pedler struck up a wild uncontrolled lilt which beat upon their ears in an almost fearful manner. After a little while he left the barn and marched down the hill towards the sea, playing his pipes. Behind him walked the men, some unsteady on their feet, some silent and some angry.

Hamish entered the Manse by the kitchen door, closing it behind him.

"Is my supper ready?" he said quietly, his voice still quivering with rage, his forehead flushed.

Bella hurried away in search of food.

He walked slowly towards the front of the house, entered his study and closed the door. In the darkness of the hall Allison stood dismayed. She yearned to comfort him, yet how could one comfort a figure of stone? How could one touch those hands that seemed not to feel, or look into those eyes which seemed blind with anger and pain?

Presently she pushed open the study door timidly. He was sitting in his leather armchair beside the fire; he had fetched his writing materials from his desk, and was working on the kirk accounts; his quill pen seemed suspended over the page. He did not raise his eyes as she advanced towards him.

"Your supper is ready, Hamish," she said gently. She laid her hand on his arm. "Why, my dear, how wet you are! Won't you change your clothes?" He did not answer, and she felt like some lonely soul shut outside the gates of the world. She struggled with her rising hysteria; her nerves were strained to breaking-point.

"I'll go upstairs and get some dry clothes ready for you," she went on doggedly. He did not answer, but only nodded his head. She turned wearily from him towards the door, and then above the noise of the wind climbed the scream of those exultant pipes, rising and falling in the darkness.

He raised his head like a trapped animal; an expression of fear and utter weariness passed over his face and he bowed his head.

In a moment she was at his side, kneeling on the floor before him. "My dear—my dear," she murmured, gently stroking his hair. She knew now that in spite of everything he needed her loyalty, if not her love. He did not speak for a little while, and when he raised his head his eyes were soft with unshed tears.

"It was after they had partaken of the Lord's Supper," he said brokenly; "and for a month I had believed that they had seen or felt the unseen Spirit; I had rejoiced—" He broke off abruptly. They sat in the gloom in silence whilst she stroked his hand gently.

Then, as he sat with his hand in hers she felt a change come over him. His hand moved restlessly, and looking up into his face she saw that the weariness had gone from his eyes.

"What is a month?" he exclaimed eagerly, and the theatrical resonance came back to his voice once more. "They shall know the truth and it is I that shall teach it to them." His voice quivered with the intensity of his feeling; he moved Allison's hand gently and stood up.

"I think I'll change my clothes before I have my supper," he said quietly, the light still shining in his eyes; and so he left her.

"Unto thee, O my strength, will I sing." Unaccountably the line of the Psalm hurried its way across Allison's mind; she repeated it sadly to herself, thinking of the moment when she had held his hand so gently in her own.

Chapter VI

Allison's baby was born the day after Christmas. Hamish was away from the house at the time, visiting some outlying crofts, where an old woman lay dying. There had been no snow at Christmas, only the interminable rain. The Manse stood like a lonely creature, cut off from the world by a wall of mist and ever-falling darkness.

The baby was born about midnight, and still Hamish had not returned. Bella had despatched John through the darkness to fetch the doctor from Strathnairn, which lay northward about nine miles from Glenlee. It took John a considerable time to reach his destination, jogging along on the back of the farm horse. The burns were high, and in places the water spread over the road two or three feet deep. The horse's hooves sank into the sodden peat, and this delayed its progress. The mist crowded in behind, accentuating the loneliness and vagueness of the country. When he reached Strathnairn, the doctor was out, there was little

chance of his returning that night. So it was
that Bella delivered the child as best she might.

Allison lay exhausted, the life in her flickering very low. To her dazed eyes the walls of
the room seemed to be closing in upon her, and
an iron band was bound round her head. The
remembrance of those waves of pain which had
enveloped her, turned her to water, and she lay,
the mere echo of human life. The thought of
death, now that the reality seemed so near, did
not trouble her; she thought no longer of the
wet clay on her dead hands, or the loneliness
of the kirkyard. She longed only for perfect
peace and inertia, freed from the suffering
which seemed unendurable, and which must
yet be endured.

Through the drowsy mist which seemed to
envelop her, the face of Bella appeared and disappeared, clear-cut against the melting background, as though carved in high-colored cedar-
wood. Then she slept.

When she awoke it was daylight. A cold
scattering of light crept through the window,
the square of which was gray and opalescent, as
though a vast eternity lay stretching into space
just beyond the solitary Manse. A strand of
ivy tapped furtively at the closed panes, the

leaves black and concrete against the gray vagueness of the sky.

A fire burned in the grate, throwing a flickering orange upon the side of the great bed where she lay. She had wakened at the sound of the door opening. Hamish stood in the doorway. His face was whipped to a fine bright color by the rain; his hair was tossed by the wind, which gave his head an even more massive appearance than usual. Eagerly he advanced into the room on tiptoe; she watched him through her half-closed eyes. He gave a quick glance towards the bed, and then advanced to the cot, which stood at the foot of it. She watched him draw back the coverlet and stoop over his son. There was an expression of mystic satisfaction upon his face which was quite indescribable; for a moment he remained in this attitude, and then he threw back his head and stood gazing out of the window into the grayness beyond. She felt that he was praying, attempting to express the rapture which swept through his soul.

She uttered his name very low. He turned slowly and came towards the bed; he took her hand. "How are you now, my dear?" he said in hushed tones, regarding her with a quivering kind of tenderness.

Suddenly she felt that she had no answer for him. She closed her eyes wearily.

"You've seen the baby? A son—" she said tonelessly. He was overcome with emotion for a moment, and could only hold her hand against the roughness of his coat. Then he began to talk in hushed tones about the doctor's being absent from Strathnairn, and of his anxiety for the baby—and for her. But she could not listen; a mechanical contraption of the cogs and wheels in mills of which she had seen pictures, seemed to be grinding inside her head. She felt nothing but the force of a life machine, a soulless producer of life, and more life, forever and ever.

Allison recovered gradually, and the baby thrived, contrary to the laws of science, according to which at least some ill effects should have been derived from Bella's lack of experience in midwifery.

The weather continued wet and dark, and the square Manse was never free from the echo of the wind in the chimneys, and the tapping of the ivy on the windows.

Hamish toiled night and day among his people; ever since the night in the barn his efforts had been redoubled. He slept alone, so that his coming to bed late into the night should

not disturb his wife. Allison saw him sometimes at meals, and on the Sabbath when she
sat in the cold gray church beneath the pulpit.
He seemed to be fading away into a dream-like
past, and all that was left was the gigantic figure
which must not be disturbed at study or while
writing sermons, and which must have hot food
at any hour on demand.

Allison was afraid of Glenlee; she attempted
to laugh herself out of the fear, but it remained,
especially at night when the mist came swooping
down, and the sea became furtive and black,
moving uneasily as though there were some
restive spirit beneath struggling for release.
The darkness always seemed to her to be utterly
void and lonely and yet pulsing with some mysterious life. She would often experience the
sensation of being watched, so that she would
arrive home cold and white with apprehension.

One night she had been out visiting a sick
woman who lived in a small croft beyond the
clump of Glenlee crofts. She had sat there
longer than she wished, reading the Bible to the
sick woman slowly and quietly, for the English
tongue was strange to many of the inhabitants
of Glenlee. The woman had insisted on the
Book of Job; she lay back with closed eyes lis-

tening to the rise and fall of Allison's clear voice,
with a look of peace on her face.

"In thoughts from the visions of the night,
when deep sleep falleth on man, fear came
upon me, and trembling, which made all my
bones to shake. Then a spirit passed before
my face; the hair of my flesh stood up. It
stood still, but I could not discern the form
thereof. An image was before mine eyes,
there was a silence—and I heard a voice."

Allison's voice died into the silence. Then
she closed the Bible and rose softly to her feet,
her gown making a little rustling noise as it settled in new folds. She bade the woman good-
night, gathered her cloak more closely round
her, and opening the cottage door found herself standing on a moonlit seashore.

It was a long time since there had been moonlight. The beauty of the scene made her catch
her breath. The croft behind her threw a
sharply defined shadow onto the rough road-
way and the beach. The stones were white and
glistening in the moonshine, round like skulls.
An edge of light fringed the darkness of the sea,
as it broke on the stones. A pathway of bril-
liancy led across the water. On her right a
stunted haystack was transformed by silver light.

She hastened along the shore path, watching the black clouds tearing across the face of the moon, plunging the earth into darkness, then splashing it with light. She watched the rim of light round the curved edges of the clouds gleaming from the moon behind.

She hurried up the glen road towards the Manse, and once more the darkness seemed alive with movement. Twice she thought she saw the dim shape of a man cross her path. She thought of that first night when she had sat alone in the gig waiting for Hamish to secure the key of the empty Manse, but in her heart of hearts she knew that there were no men abroad in the glens.

She stumbled up to the Manse, breathless and trembling. The moonlight shone on the square of the door until it was like a slab of gray light. A dark shadow was cast from the knocker, which gave some substantiality to the effect of the door's transparency.

Allison beat her hands against the panels repeatedly; she dared not turn her head. A dark leaf fluttered to her feet. The "shape" or "image" of the Book of Job haunted her imagination. She beat more loudly on the door. She heard steps approaching, and the light of a candle shone out through the hall window. She could scarcely bear to wait; she almost staggered against the door.

She heard the chain removed and the door opened. She thrust herself in, catching the door and slamming it behind her. Only then did she notice that it was Hamish who held the candle. She had not expected him home so early.

"Why, Allison!" he exclaimed, holding the candle aloft so that the light might fall on her. "Whatever ails you?" He stretched out his hand and laid it on her trembling arm.

"Oh, nothing, nothing," she faltered nervously, pulling the mittens on and off her small numbed hands.

"But, my dear," insisted Hamish, leading her towards the open study door, "you're trembling. Did something frighten you?"

He led her to the green leather armchair by the fire, and stood above her waiting for an answer. She looked up into his face, which was kindly in the firelight.

"Oh, Hamish," she said wildly, "there's something about the hills at night—I can't stand them—I can't bear the feeling of their laughter—"

"Their laughter?" he interrogated, puzzled.

"Yes, their laughter—their laughter because of our petty and ridiculous impermanence here; they gloat over us, standing out there mingled with the rain and the wind."

"My dear," Hamish said quietly, "you mustn't give way to these nervous fears; you know that the mountains are God's work, but they have no soul. True, they remain, whereas we pass," he continued after a moment's thought, "but they remain soulless; we pass on into a life immortal. Their permanence is as nothing to our immortality." He spoke patiently, as if reasoning with an overwrought child.

"How do we know? How do we know?" cried Allison wildly; her recent terror had broken down her reserve. "How do we know that we inherit life immortal? The age of the mountains is proved to us—where is the proof of our immortality?"

Hamish had walked a few paces across the room. He turned quickly and stood gazing at her; until that moment he had treated her fears as mere womanish fancies born of the darkness, but now he heard the anguish of real terror in her voice. He was dumfounded. How do we know we are immortal? What is the proof?

These were strange questions for Allison, his own wife, to ask. His face grew stern.

"Allison," he said, "in the Holy Book we are promised immortality; is that sufficient proof for you?"

She was trembling now; why had she cried out in that strange way? What had she said about the mountains and immortality? She had not meant that at all; it was the dark figures she thought she had seen which had frightened her. She hung her head and could not speak.

He raised her to her feet. "Allison," he said slowly, "never say a thing like that again. It is terrible blasphemy; if you deny immortality you deny your consciousness of a soul. The unbeliever shall be consumed by fire."

She did not follow him, but she saw the grief and horror in his eyes, and also anger, which made her tremble. "Yes, Hamish," she faltered very low. Persistently a voice within her whispered, "And if I should think it?" But she did not listen. She left the room slowly.

Hamish sat on in the firelight, his head leaning on his hand. He was weary of the struggle against the overwhelming odds which had assailed him ever since the beginning of his ministry at Glenlee. The people were hostile, their poverty and their morals were shameful, he had worked in vain to produce some spark of divine fire from them.

At times he had been oppressed, as Allison had been, by the space and power of the mountains and the sea; he was but an infinitesimal atom, like some tiny futile ant dragging a minute straw along behind it. The ant and the straw, he and his beliefs, what purpose could they serve in the gigantic scale of the universe?

His eyes fell on the sermon which lay beside him, half finished. Written across the top, in his firm, sloping hand, was the text from St. Luke's Gospel from which it was to be preached.

Then said Jesus, Father, forgive them, for they know not what they do.

Pity surged through him; but pity was an inactive emotion, pity must be coupled with courage and unflagging determination. He sat straight in his chair once more and took up his sermon. Allison had gone from his mind. There was silence in the study save for the whistle of the wind in the chimney and the scratch of his pen.

Chapter VII

As the winter pursued its sodden despairing course, covering the world with darkness from the hours of three till eight, Allison's spirits began to revive. She ceased to be haunted by the immensity of the mountains and the sea, she ceased to lament the loss of Hamish's companionship. A calm seemed to have descended upon her, a passiveness which caused her to pass through life with a certain quiet joy. Sometimes she was happy. This was when she was playing with her children, or telling them stories to keep them silent lest they should disturb Hamish.

Jean was nearing six years of age. Her life was composed of a series of thrills of joy and horror, born of a vivid imagination. The world in which she lived was full of mysteries. For instance, there was the vast cupboard in the room at the back of the house where she slept with Bella. This cupboard reached to the very ceiling of the room, and was filled with shelves set close together, almost like the steps of a ladder, but should she by any chance set foot on this tempting ladder, down would come the immense cupboard—Bella had told her so. She would be pinioned under it forever and ever. She always hoped to herself that the actual shelves would miss her; she could probably squeeze in between them, she thought, and there she would lie forever, until at last she would die of starvation. Perhaps if Bella poured some milk through the crack between the cupboard and the floor, she might really be able to live forever, and Mama would come and read to her on the other side of the cupboard. She hoped that Mama would read about Aladdin's cave, and not about Christian or about Adamaneve, or Jacobanesau. She preferred Aladdin because she always thought that it would be quite easy to find the magic cave round the northern headland, to which she intended to make a journey some day; thus the story had a double interest. The reading, however, would be sure to deal with Adamaneve or Jacobanesau; these were the stories that Mama liked, apparently, and although it was difficult to imagine Adamaneve on the slopes of Ben Buie, it could be done.

After all, the Adamaneve type of story was

much to be preferred to the stories in "A Sunday Book for Boys and Girls," which related the misdeeds and punishments of the strangest boys and girls, who ended their lives by being "hanged by the neck." One day she had asked Mama what it meant to be "hanged by the neck." Mama had not answered at first, and then she had said: "It is something that is done to wicked people who do not love the Lord."

They had been sitting in Papa's study, and Papa himself sat in his green leather chair opposite. When he heard Mama say this, he had looked up from his book and said: "Tell her the truth, my dear; never hide the reward of sin from a child, however young."

Mama had said, "Oh, Hamish!" in a way that made Jean want to cry, because of some instinctive sympathy. Then Papa told her to come over to him and he had held her between his knees. Her eyes had been level with his great gold watch-chain; she could not help wondering if the gold of which it was made had been dug out of a mountainside by little men in peaked caps who held lanterns and pickaxes. (Bella had often told her of these little men, though, to be sure, she always added: "But, och! it's all havers.")

"Jean," Papa had said in his kirk voice, "if you are wicked and disobey God's commandments, people will take you, tie a rope round your neck and hang you up on a post, and you will die. When you are dead you will go down to Hell with other sinners, and you will be burnt forever and ever."

She had not listened very carefully, because she was thinking about the little men with the pickaxes, but she heard the part about being burnt forever and ever. She knew what it was to be burnt, because there was a large fender round the fire in the nursery which had brass bars. These became almost red-hot when the fire had been lit some time. Once she had seized a shining bar in her fingers. The skin had come off, and she had been so hurt that she could not even cry out; so she knew all about burning. The idea of being burnt all over with all the other people called "sinners" filled her with horror; it was all the more terrible because of the assurance she had obtained from Bella that Mama would not be in Hell, and that, in all probability, Fergus McGeachy, who lived all alone in a cottage higher up the glen road, would be. Fergus had broken teeth, and Jean thought that he probably ate people. She saw

him sometimes walking slowly up the road, with
a sack upon his shoulders.

John had said once to her, "Mind ye now,
and be a guid girl, else McGeachy will tak ye
awa' in his muckle great sack." She had not
liked to ask John whether McGeachy ate his
victims, but she supposed that he did. Somehow the picture of Moses in the illustrated
Bible reminded her of McGeachy, especially
the one of his casting the tablets of the law
down the hillside. Whenever Mama began to
read about Moses, Jean would beseech her not
to, and would turn over the picture with a
podgy but determined hand.

"But, my dear," Mama would always say,
"Moses was a very kind, good man, and he
helped all the poor children of Israel to escape
from the cruel Egyptians." But still Jean was
suspicious of Moses, and Mama did not read to
her about him, or insist upon her looking at
that hideous picture of Fergus McGeachy and
the stone tablets.

But of all the mysteries that puzzled the small
mind of Jean, that of "the Lord" Himself was
the most baffling. He appeared to be everywhere; He saw you when you thought that
there was no one there, and every night you said

prayers to Him, and every meal you ate you said Grace to Him, and yet you never saw Him as you saw Papa or Captain Fraser the factor, or Sir Ian the laird. He lived in Heaven, which was all golden. But the mystery did not stop there, because there was Jesus, who was his son, who was kind to every one, but Jesus was also God. Then there was something still more mysterious called "the Holy Ghost," and that was God, too.

Once or twice Jean had sought enlightenment from Mama, but Mama had only said, "Why, Jeanie, never mind just now; you'll understand when you're older."

God lived in the kirk by the sea as well as in Heaven. Papa had told her so; he had said, "Jean, this is God's house." She supposed that God just visited this house, leaving His own mansions in Heaven for a short period. She had never actually seen Him in the church, but she supposed that He remained behind the door through which Papa disappeared after he had finished the service.

The Lord, she always thought, must be a mixture between the pictures in the illustrated Bible and Papa himself— His voice, she was certain, would be like Papa's, and when He sent "sinners" to burn, she thought He would shout angrily, as Papa sometimes did in the pulpit. She supposed that He would know all the Psalms by heart, and the shorter Catechism, and would send the "sinners" to Hell because they made a mistake in recitation when they arrived in Heaven. She would be sure to make a mistake, she thought; she would be so frightened. Every Sabbath evening she had to recite to Papa and the words would fly from her mind. Mama would sit mouthing at her, but she could never make out what she said, and she dared not look at Papa. Then suddenly she would burst out crying, and Mama would run forward and stroke her hair just as though she were a little ill-used animal. All the time Papa would be silent, and Mama's eyes were often full of tears as well as Jean's.

These were some of Jean's particular horrors; sometimes they appeared so immense and terrifying that her mind was paralyzed and she would lie in the vast bed which she shared with Bella, her eyes tightly closed; she dared not open them lest she should see a flaming devil before her, or Fergus McGeachy and his sack. At night when the Manse was silent and mysterious, a feeling of unbearable loneliness

would creep over her. Far away down the long
expanse of stairs, the doors into the study and
into the kitchen premises cut her off from all
human aid. There was no light save a dull
flicker which was cast from the candles in the
hall beneath. Through the narrow aperture
of the bedroom door, which was left ajar, she
could discern dimly the unlit landing.

The Manse itself seemed inhabited at this
time by strange forms, and the sound of these
mysterious movements filled her ears; ever and
anon the head of Fergus McGeachy would peep
stealthily round the door, silhouetted sharply
against the strip of dim light. And then it
would be stealthily withdrawn and she would
hear footsteps creeping away across the landing. Once his figure had filled the whole doorway, and Jean had screamed with fear. She
had seemed to be sinking down and down into
a dark pit. Mama had come running up the
stairs with a candle trembling in her hand, the
smoke streaming out in the draught. The
comfort of her presence and the feel of her
cheek, which was soft in an inexpressible way,
made the child cling to her as though all the
horrors of darkness were still around her.
Mama had sung to her, and rocked her to and

fro, and then Papa had come into the room. The sound of his voice seemed to shatter the soft film of whispering unity which had enveloped Allison and the child.

"Is the child ill?" he inquired, resting his hand on the edge of the bed. "You left the door open, my dear, when you came upstairs, and my papers were blown all over the study." His tone was weary and reproachful.

Allison laid the child back in the bed, and turned to go with Hamish. "I'll fetch Bella," she said; "the child has been dreaming, and was trembling with fear when I found her."

Hamish had turned from her; his voice was almost harsh with weariness.

"Let the child be," he said; "dreams are only dreams. She is quiet now." He stooped over the bed. "The Lord will take care of you, Jeanie; say your prayers and He will give you rest," and then he took away the light and the darkness flowed back into the room, and the Devil and Fergus McGeachy began to creep about the house once more.

She had prayed to the Lord, trying to imagine Him with a protecting arm like that of Mama, but the Lord became inexplicably mixed up with a vision of Papa, and Jean grew afraid as

she did when she had to say her Catechism.
Then she sobbed quietly because she was a
"sinner" and disobeyed her father.

These terrors, however, only swept over her
in the darkening hours, also sometimes when
she was shut up alone in the cupboard beneath
the stairs after she had been particularly dis-
obedient. At other times the joy of existence
seemed to radiate from her firm little body.
Her shining gray eyes would light up suddenly
as though some door had been swung open in
her mind when she gazed on anything that
pleased her.

She had a passion for animals, and would
cherish a wounded bird with the utmost tenderness until it died and filled her with an unas-
suageable sorrow. She would play for hours
with the old gray cat and Hamish's spaniel, Lo-
chy. At the sight of the rabbits which scuttered about the side of Ben Buie, she would
stretch out her little hands in an ecstasy, longing to fondle them. Flowers she loved in a
fierce kind of way. She would gather them
greedily, and squeeze them in her hands, pressing them to her small nose and mouth; and
running to Allison she would cram them

against her mother's face, crying, "Smell. Smell."

There was a stunted lilac bush that struggled for existence in the Manse garden. In the spring, the delicate star-shaped little blossoms appeared in their beautiful conical formation. Jean had found them, and had torn them eagerly from the tree. The scent was almost more than she could bear. She wanted to shout and dance, she ran with all her might through the shadows of the trees surrounding the Manse, her small legs in their long pantaloons twinkling in the dim light. In through the front door she sped to the parlor, where Allison sat with her embroidery-frame in the window. She flung her hot little body against her, and with an eager and flushed face raised to Allison's, she pressed the blossoms to her mother's mouth. Then she broke away, dancing and humming to herself, stretching out her hands to catch the motes that floated down the sunbeams which came in through the window, and holding out her muslin skirt.

Allison watched her. She felt as though her own spirit had left her and was sharing an elemental joy with the child. Then she glanced at the crushed blossoms in the little clenched hand; the bright tender green of the leaves was bruised and one of the flowers hung broken.

"But, my sweet," she said softly, "the poor flower is crumpled and it will die. Why did you pull it from its green tree where it could feel the sun and look at the sea and the hills?"

The child stopped in the middle of her dance, her attention arrested. She turned her inquiring gaze on Allison. "It smelt so lovely, Mama," she said in eager explanation.

"But it won't smell any more now," explained Allison; "it will go brown and its flowers will drop off. It will die, my darling."

But the child could not understand; she clasped the blossoms once again and danced away into the rare sunlight outside.

She would play for hours in the little hazel copse at the back of the Manse. Sometimes she would take Alex with her, but his legs were so stout and short that he was liable to fall among the mosses and cover his clothes with green stains, and then Bella would be angry.

In this copse the scenes of the Old Testament were enacted. Here Abraham led Isaac to the sacrifice, and here Isaac lay in surprised discomfort on a pile of damp sticks, waiting for Jeanie to release him. At the corner of the copse was a great whin bush. Once Allison had said, "Look, Jeanie, at that beautiful bush, just as though it were on fire with sunlight," and Jean had looked up and said, "Like Moses' bush, Mama." Allison had not been sure whether she should reassure her daughter on this point, so she had diverted her attention.

But in the spring Jean would pad round the bush in her little cotton stockings, leaving her shoes in the copse, and she would hear the voice of God from the whin bush. Then she must leave this world of the copse and face Bella with her mud-sodden white stockings, and then she would be sure to tell a wicked lie and Bella would say: "Guid Sakes!" and Mama's eyes would fill with tears, and Papa would beat her with a folded newspaper, and shut her up in the cupboard. The beating did not hurt her, but the cupboard ate into her soul, and at night the Devil would peep round the door, waiting to take her to Hell to be burnt and burnt.

No one knew what scenes were enacted in the copse; not even Mama could guess. Sometimes Alex made inopportune remarks, but he was so small, and he laughed and chuckled so much when he spoke that nobody listened to him.

Allison's children were a growing sense of delight to her. They represented to her a hard nucleus from which grew the justification for existence. Although she did not realize it, there was nothing in which she believed with so much intensity. In a world of unsubstantial theories and ideals, the children seemed the only proofs of reality. They were there; they were part of her, yet they were separate souls. They were mystery and reality combined.

It was easier to think of God, and the making of the world, and of miracles, when there was some concrete proof before the eyes. Allison hardly realized that she felt like this about her children, but occasionally, when she lay in bed at night, waiting for Hamish to return from some late visit, the wonder of the miracle of procreation of both spirit and body would come over her, and she would rejoice, and creeping from the great four-poster bed, catch her baby out of its cot, and hold it to her, just to feel the movement of life in it.

Hamish was becoming more and more engaged in his ministerial duties, and the Allison who had once sorrowed because she could no longer feel the ecstasy of his arm around her in the darkness, was appeased by the unadulterated love of her children and their elemental joy in her presence. She was happy as she had not been since the first year of her marriage, and it was rare now that she was filled with that indefinable longing and uncertainty which had overwhelmed her before the birth of David, the last baby. When that sense of unfulfilment swept over her, there was no comfort, and the tears filled her eyes when she looked at her children, because of an ineffable pathos in their innocence and trust, and because of the hopelessness of discovering the terrible inspiring "nothing" which remained invisible forever, hidden behind clouds which were always moving, so that occasionally their density lessened, and the ineffable gleam of glory penetrated.

CHAPTER VIII

SPRING in the Highlands
makes up for its tardy appearance by its freshness. It is no long-drawn-out preparation for
summer, when the dust may sully the joy of the
leaves, but a short, sudden rebirth; in May the
snow still gleams on the hill-tops, then the earth
rejoices in June as only earth shrouded in darkness, frost and rain for six months of the year
can rejoice.

Through April and May, Allison had felt
unconsciously the revival of life. It seemed to
her afterwards that spring must have come
much more beautifully that year than in any
other year of her life. At the beginning of May
she would climb the southern headland to look
out across the moorland which lay beyond. In
the distance she could see the blue of the driven
rain, scudding across the stretches of moor, but
in front of her the country was bathed in a
fitful yellowish light, dotted and slashed with
dark scars where the heather had been burnt
away in preparation for the laird's grouse shoot-

ing in August. In the distance rose the Knoydart hills, so dark a purple as to be almost black;
faintly against them the fairylike blue of smoke
from the burning heather was outlined as it
stretched itself across the blackness, torn and
straggled by the wind. The sea stretched in
silent silver, and the vast piles of rambling
clouds seemed everlasting. Everywhere she
could smell and see the damp, oozing and rich,
deepening the color of last year's orange beech
leaves which clung to the hedge up by the
Manse. The yellow light caressed the green of
the larches down by the burn, so that it seemed
as though they were soft luscious things, instead of the hardy, spiked creatures that they
are in reality. At night when she went to bed,
and the profound listening silence of the glen
swept downward, she would sometimes hear
the startled pipe of a whaup or an oyster-
catcher as it settled itself for the night.

It seemed to her afterwards that she had
known subconsciously that she was waiting for
something which should be a fulfilment of herself, and for which she had been waiting all her
life. Something was coming to her which
would explain the glory, and yet the baffling
inevitability of human existence.

It was one evening in June that Andrew Simon came to the Manse.

Allison had been down to visit one of the crofters after supper, and then she had climbed the southern headland to gaze out over the sunset lying behind the hills of the Islands. Between the hills and the headland, the sound lay dark, unfathomable in its depth, gleaming with a deep gold fire. She had stood there for a short time, the wind ruffling her curls which had escaped from beneath her close-fitting black bonnet. With a sigh she turned and retraced her steps.

The drive up to the Manse front door seemed darker than usual after the strange glow of the sunset on the road outside; the door stood open and a shaft of clear orange light fell across the doorstep, dyeing the fronds of ivy which encroached upon it, to gold. The blank windows of the little square house blazed fiercely in the sunset. Through the door came the sound of a man's voice. She knew at once that it could not be that of Hamish, for she had seen him down on the shore, talking to the fishermen as they mended their nets.

She entered the hall timidly, clutching her mauve shawl more closely to her, for the heat had made her throw it back from her shoulders.

He was talking to Bella in the hall; he turned as she entered and moved towards her. He bowed slightly, and then began to speak in that husky, eager voice that she was to know so well.

He apologized for his presence: he was an artist touring the Highlands, and his supply of provisions had been exhausted sooner than he expected. He wondered if he might crave the hospitality of the Manse.

Timidly she replied that her husband would be delighted to entertain him; would he not sleep the night with them?

He said that he would not trouble her, he was used to sleeping out of doors. He threw back his head and laughed in a strange chuckling kind of way.

"My husband is down by the sea," said Allison. "Won't you come down, Mr—Mr.—" She faltered, being unacquainted with his name.

"Simon," he replied, smiling down on her; "Andrew Simon." And he bowed again, a gesture that went oddly with his rough untidy clothes.

They walked out into the glow of the sunset again, and Allison saw that he was of short stature. His skin was bronzed and he wore a low linen collar with no stock. He had an abundant crop of dark hair, touched at the temples with gray. A lock of it hung down over his brow. His eyes were a clear greenish hazel; they were penetrating, so that his gaze filled her with confusion. There were lines at the corners of his eyes, yet he had a curiously boyish expression.

For the first time she noticed that he limped, and that his left hand lacked two fingers. He walked with a slouching shamble, almost a run; it was all she could do to keep up with him, as he raced down the hill road to the sea. He was talking all the time, indicating this and that with his right hand. She was too out of breath, and too agitated, to listen to his discourse. Occasionally he would dart a sudden look at her, his face breaking into a smile, so that she smiled back at him, hoping that he would not notice how out of breath she was.

She carried a basket on her arm, in which there had been some bread which she had distributed among the crofters.

Suddenly he stopped short, and with a quick darting movement, seized the basket from her arm.

"How thoughtless of me!" he exclaimed,

holding the basket out in front of him as though
it were responsible for his misdemeanor. "And
you've been carrying it all this way, and I was
so busy talking I never even noticed—and you're
out of breath, too—my long strides—they always
get me into trouble—why, ma'am, you're quite
exhausted; it's always the same, always looking
so far ahead that I can't see the things at my
feet."

He paused for a moment. "Now, I've been
looking at that—" he waved the basket vaguely
towards the hills of the Islands and the flaring
yellow of the sky behind them, "and so I never
saw you, who were just beside me." He looked
down, smiling.

Allison was bewildered. She had never heard
any one speak quite so inconsequently before.
She wished that he would go on and stop holding out her basket in front of him and gazing
down on her as though she were a beetle that
he had suddenly discovered in the moss.

"I'm always losing things because of my ab-
sent-mindedness," he continued, still standing
in the middle of the road. "That's how I lost
my palette knife this morning—it was in my
hand all the time, until I actually began to climb
the rocks to see better, and then I found there

was something in the way so that I couldn't grip, so I put it down—and when I reached the top there was the most wonderful stretch of blue and purple and green and—a sort of gray that cannot be described—but no palette knife!"

He laughed again, and because his laugh was infectious, and because she did not know what else to do, she laughed, as well.

He offered her his arm and proceeded solemnly and slowly over the rough stones. Once he stopped, and craving her pardon with his odd little bow, he stooped down and picked a flower of red campion from the grass at the side of the road. He held it in his hand, as though it were some rare treasure. Then he held it towards her almost as Jean might have done. The curves of the little petals as they met together in their bulbous formation seemed to fascinate him; he pointed this out to her eagerly. Then he put the flower back into the dew-wet grass at the roadside.

She watched him, wondering.

"I always do that," he explained, taking her arm again, "because if I keep it in my buttonhole or pressed in a book," he patted his pocket, which bulged awkwardly with the sharp corners of a book, "it dies, and then I cannot help but

think of its aliveness and then—of its deadness."
He paused a moment and a cloud passed over
his face. He continued more slowly. "It's a
horrible thought—'deadness,'" he said, "especially if you consider 'aliveness' at the same time
—don't you think so?" He darted the question
at her suddenly.

Unaccountably her mind stirred to the
thought that had haunted her before the birth
of her last baby, the thought of the clay on her
own small hands; involuntarily she stretched
them forward a little.

"Yes," she said very low, and she looked up at
him curiously, but she saw that his mind was off
on another tack, for Hamish was approaching
them, his figure black, silhouetted against the
sunset.

It seemed to Allison that she had known this
man a long time; he had said so much in so
short a time.

Hamish was delighted at the thought of a
visitor; his eager and intelligent mind fretted
under the restrictions of this out-of-the-world
parish, and he longed to discuss the problems
of government, the growing industrialism, the
rights of the people, and endless other subjects
which filled his mind from time to time. It

was unfortunate, of course, that Simon was an artist; he had never actually known an artist before, but he had always heard that they were queer customers, often immoral. But he liked the look of this one, with his straightforward darting glance, polished bearing and his way of listening intently while Hamish was speaking.

As the three strolled towards the Manse once more, it was gloaming; the western sky had lost its luminous light and lay as a faint yellow haze, fast fading to gray, the light dulling the outlines of the hills which had stood silhouetted so sharply against the sunset a quarter of an hour earlier. An owl flew silently across the road, and in the distance the lonely cry of a whaup disturbed the silence for a moment. A buzzard wheeled and hovered above the rocks. The dew lay heavy on the grass, and the air was filled with the damp indefinable smell of evening, a heavy drugging smell, sharpened only by the tang of salt.

"You will find it very beautiful here," said Hamish. "The sea itself is enough study for a lifetime; the shadows on the hills, too, are wonderful in the summer months. Do you paint landscapes, Mr. Simon?"

Simon had been listening intently to the tones

of Hamish's beautiful voice, which seemed to express the silence rather than break it. He had not understood the import of the words themselves. Now there was a pause in the quiet deep music of the voice; no doubt some answer was expected of him.

"Have you ever thought how revealing the darkness must be to an owl?" he said eagerly. "To sit all day with light blazing over everything, so that there is nothing—nothing but one insufferable glare, and then the coming of a beautiful grayness with the mysterious forms of things appearing which did not exist in the dazzle of daylight, and the realization of vast tracts of earth over which to fly, and then the sea—" He ceased abruptly, smiling uncertainly at Hamish, then he continued in his husky cultivated voice, "But I think you asked me a question, sir? You must pardon my verbosity."

Hamish repeated his question once more, but he did not add his remarks as to the changeable beauty of the sea and of the shadows; they seemed empty and not worthy of the intent interest which Simon had switched upon them, like a penetrating ray of light.

The evening passed pleasantly enough. Hamish, eager for the news of the doings of men, plied his guest with questions, which he answered to the best of his ability. He was a good conversationalist and his career had been a varied one; he was no lonely recluse. He brought the streets of London, with the gay throng of carriages, beautiful women and fashionable rakes of men before the eyes of the young minister, for the gray cloud of Victorianism had not yet settled over England. He had traveled in France and Switzerland; he described the cities abroad in a few vivid words, so that Hamish burned with a desire to see them for himself, to roam the world untrammeled by circumstances. There was something about Andrew Simon, who seemed half poet, half man of the world, which drew forth hidden fires in Hamish and stirred desires in him which had long lain dormant.

They spoke of Brussels. Simon's face clouded and he pushed back the thick hair restlessly from his forehead. "I do not like to think of it for long," he said slowly. "I cannot think of it without hearing the distant roar of the cannons seventeen years ago, and the everlasting clatter of horses—horses—horses over the cobbles of the streets, going towards coldness and death. It was all so horrible—the brightness of the ball-

room, as though it could never end, as though
the shining walls were the edges of a world—
as though life went on forever—and then—the
summer night outside and the wind and that
clatter of horses."

"Were you campaigning at the time of Quatre
Bras and Waterloo, then?" asked Hamish
quietly, for he saw a strange hard expression on
Simon's face.

"Yes," he replied slowly.

There was a pause. Simon rose, and, drawing the curtain aside, gazed out into the night.
The daylight still lingered, but the moon had
risen, and the light was falling in clear shafts
across the drive; the vast black shadows moved
as the trees above swayed in the wind which
came up from the sea. The moonlight delighted him; he turned from the window smiling, smoothing back his unruly lock of hair.

"How clear the shadows are in the moonlight!" he said. He wandered back into the
middle of the room, fiddling with the things
on Hamish's desk and on the mantelpiece.

Later on, Allison came in to bid them good-
night. She had sat in the parlor by herself,
listening absently to the murmur of their voices
from the study. It seemed to her that she rarely

thought now; she simply passed from one thing to another, calculating how best it could be effected; and yet there was this strange unrest which she could not define. When she was left alone and there were no more household duties to be performed, she could not remain idle, and yet nothing pleased her. She would take up a book, only to lay it down once more with a sigh; she would follow the printed word upon the page and turn over page after page, but there was a persistent barrier between her senses and her understanding. She felt as though she must play upon the upright piano which stood in the corner by the window, but after she had searched out new candles and fitted them into the tarnished brass sockets, her inclination died away and she took up some embroidery.

Dreamily she imagined herself sitting in the study, listening to the conversation of the two men. She had followed their discourse as they had walked up the glen in the gloaming, and longed to hear more of London and of the dark miserable regions where children, almost as small as her own Jean, were made to work for long hours beneath the earth, dragging heavy trucks of coal. She thought she would ask Simon about the clothes worn by the ladies in

London. Somehow she felt that the inquiry
would not appear absurd to him. She could
imagine him contracting his brows and treating
the subject with characteristic eagerness and
interest. His deferential bearing towards her
flattered her. Perhaps, however, Hamish would
not like her to discuss such fripperies as laces
and muslins with any one.

She sighed, looking down with disgust at her
plain gray gown with its muslin fichu clasped
in front by a cameo brooch that had been her
mother's. Her dark hair was gathered neatly
into a roll at the back of her head. Hamish
thought curls unsuitable, so after her marriage
she had pushed them back, so that now they
had grown to the same length as the rest of her
hair and could be more easily restrained.

At eleven o'clock she rose rather wearily to
go and bid them good-night. The scene in the
peaceful firelit study stamped itself on her
mind with an extraordinary intensity. Every
detail seemed carved into her memory forever.
Afterwards, when she looked back, it seemed to
her that the curtain drawn untidily back from
the window, and the unaccustomed briarwood
pipe lying on the table with the burnt-out ash
spilling from it, were the beginning of a dream-

like era in her life which seemed afterwards to
be a figment of her own brain.

Hamish sat in his old green leather chair,
leaning forward, the light of the fire casting deep
shadows along the side of his nose and his brow.
Simon was striding up and down the room, talking rapidly in his husky hurried voice; his hands
were thrust into the pockets of his shapeless yet
jaunty coat; the lock of dark hair fell over his
left brow.

As Allison pushed upon the heavy swing door
which separated the study from the hall, he
paused in his pacing and stopped, fiddling with
the dolphin tobacco jar on the mantelpiece with
his long, rather white, fingers.

Allison stood in the circle of the lamplight
looking up at them both, for Hamish had risen
at her entry. The intent gaze of Simon filled
her with confusion; the color rose to her cheeks
as she curtsied to him. He gave her his funny
little stiff bow, and then limped over to the
door to hold it open as she passed out.

"Good-night, ma'am," he said, still gazing at
her with frank admiration.

"I hope you will find your bedroom comfortable," she said, looking up at him. "I have

given orders for a warming-pan to be left in till half-past eleven."

"Why, it will be luxurious, not comfortable," he said with a chuckle. "I have not slept in a bed for the last nine days; the night before last I was obliged to pass the night in a peat hole!"

"The night before last!" she ejaculated horror-struck. "But the rain was pitiless—you must have been soaked to the skin." Involuntarily she stretched out her hand to feel the sleeve of his coat, at which he laughed and filled her with confusion once more, but he had noticed the plumpness and whiteness of her small hand.

"Don't forget to look at the moon," he said with a smile, "and the stars in 'the heaven's wide pathless way'—'wide pathless way'!" he repeated the words softly to himself.

Hamish's voice came from the fireplace.

"You're dripping the grease from your candle upon the carpet, my dear."

"Yes, Hamish," she replied, casting down her eyes again.

Hurriedly she left them.

She undressed slowly that night, sitting on the foot of the dark four-poster bed in which she had borne three children to Hamish.   She brushed her thick dark hair.

Presently she went over to the window and drew aside the curtains.   It was scarcely dark and the moon shone brightly; straggling clouds rushed across its face like dark wisps of gauze. Then a great blooming cloud floated formlessly over it and the light shone out from the edge in a glittering rim.   Farther up, the sky was clearer; the great arch of the heavens was powdered with the tiny stars of the Milky Way. She gazed and gazed, till more and more stars appeared, and the immensity of space began to creep into her soul.   For a moment she seemed to be free, and then she felt the touch of the ivy on her fingers as they grasped the sill.   Suddenly she was cold and a little frightened.   She closed the window softly.   The walls of the room seemed to close in upon her and the vision of the Milky Way—"the heaven's wide pathless way"—lingered in her brain.

She knelt down beside the crib where David, her youngest son, lay sleeping, his small fist jammed into his soft mouth.

He was different from the other two children. His hair was dark like her own, and his eyes a deep glowing chestnut color.   He seldom smiled, but he seldom cried. There was something about him that seemed to unite him to her with a fierce bond that nothing could break. Six months ago she had lain on that dark four-poster bed overwhelmed by pain and despair, and now she knelt strong and eager beside the crib of the child that had grown up as one with her. The miracle stirred her mind once more, and she lifted the child gently from his crib that she might feel the warmth of his little body. He stirred in his sleep and she held him tighter. Covering him carefully with a blanket, she carried him to the window. Once more she threw open the casement and looked out into the immensity of the star-laden heavens. She felt the baby moving his head against her breast; she felt the agelessness of the sky, its power and inevitability.

Her eyes shone and that strange longing and glory came into her soul. Her mind was in a turmoil, tears started to her eyes.

How long she stood there she did not know. She was dimly conscious of the murmur of voices in the study below.

Presently she placed the baby in his crib and climbed into the four-poster. The bedclothes were chilly, and she herself was shivering. A frightened loneliness overcame her, so that she had to rise once more and grope towards the crib. She climbed back into bed holding the sleeping child lightly.

Gradually her loneliness faded and she slept.

CHAPTER IX

THE week that Andrew Simon
was to spend in the Manse grew into a month.
The freshness of June gave place to the staler
warmth of July. It was light for nearly twenty-
four hours; the frost seemed to have departed
forever from the night air. The hills of the
Islands were far away, divided from the main-
land by a smoke-blue gauze. The summit of
Ben Buie shimmered before the uplifted gaze.
The wild roses down by the sea were shedding
their frail petals on the breeze, revealing the
voluptuous oval of the hip beneath. The gray
of the shore was edged with the bitter sienna-
colored sorrel, and small delicately molded flags,
holding their proud heads aloft among the fresh
green spikes of their leaves; the yellow ragwort flared everywhere.

It was a hotter July than they had had in the
Highlands for twelve years. The burn at the
back of the house murmured no longer; its
course was dry, like a valley of bones. White
dust rose from the twisting road and turned

the grass of the Manse glebeland to a dark olive.

Hamish was always working. Sometimes he worked in the fields with his men, for he came of an old farming stock in Kintyre and there was a great love of the land in him; nothing pleased him better than to run his hand along the shaggy backs of his black cattle or to gather the lambs for counting.

He was having trouble with the schoolmaster, a certain James McLellan. This man had been in the parish for close on twenty years, and was well over fifty years of age. He was a scholar, and had once been a respectable enough member of the community; but twenty years of that soft mist-soaked loneliness had driven him to dreams—dreams too often traceable to frequent application to the bottle. He was a tall man, with a scholarly stoop. His hair was long, almost touching his shoulders, and he wore an old-fashioned coat with large brass buttons as big as pennies. His eyes were the most striking thing about him. They were long and narrow, and slanted downwards at the corners; over them his shaggy gray brows jutted like the hair on an old sheepdog.

Hamish hated McLellan. He despised him,

a man with a divine soul, the slave of drink, making himself into an animal, degrading him-. self before the people who were less animal and degraded in their ignorance than he himself. He personified to Hamish all the dreaming immobility of the people with whom he had to deal. This man represented the spirit against which he felt he must fight, the spirit of degraded submission to the forces of nature.

Hamish had turned to Simon one evening and with a note of weariness in his voice had said, "There is nothing to compare with this West Highland dreaming to sap the energy from men; the remoteness of the glen, shut off from the world in the winter by darkness and snow, leaves the inhabitants nothing but imagination. Imagination can never satisfy the whole of a man's mind, it only takes away his grip on reality. He cannot understand true religion; he cannot realize himself as the possessor of a divine spirit; the importance of life is lost to him. To interest him, his imagination must be fired, he clings to relics and charms which he hangs about his neck to keep off evil spirits. These are the things with which he attempts to satisfy himself; there must be no need to think, no need to struggle. Sometimes the visualizing faculty of imagination makes life unbearable, and it must be either stimulated to beauty or smothered by the intoxicating fumes of whisky."

Yet McLellan was no worse than many of the schoolmasters in the Highlands at the time, and Hamish, try as he would, could lay upon no real proof of inefficiency to report to headquarters. The people, too, were attached in their strange aloof manner to the old man. He wrote their letters for them, and generally transacted any business involving figures, in return for a glass of whisky. They were quite ready to set their children to school under him. Once again Hamish fought his battle alone.

It was on the subject of McLellan that Hamish and Simon first disagreed. For a month they had delighted in each other's company, and both looked forward to the evening, when they would sit before the peat fire in Hamish's study and argue about the rights of mankind in general. Their basic ideas were entirely different, Hamish dwelling on the natural corrupt state of man which must be fought against and conquered, and Simon, in spite of his thirty-five years and rather cynical outlook, insisting on the Rousseauistic doctrine of man's natural "goodness," and the weaving of vice into his nature by the oppression of men-made institutions. Hamish's Old Testament doctrines and complete faith in the Word of God left Simon amazed, but he offered no argument upon religious themes, reveling rather in Hamish as a complete uplifted spirit, than in the details of his state of ideal elevation. Often the conversation drew nearer and nearer to the brink of disaster; as, for instance, in the case of the discussion with regard to man's primary nature. The words of the Bible flowed from Hamish's lips as freely as his own.

After five minutes' heated argument upon man's essential goodness, with regard to McLellan, there came a pause in the conversation. Hamish suddenly felt as though he were being assailed by an unknown thing. He looked searchingly at Simon, who lounged opposite him, his eyes satirical.

Hamish spoke slowly, in his deep resonant voice. "We are sinners," he said, "born in evilness, but we shall live perfect through Christ in the life hereafter. 'I am the Resurrection and the Life; he that believeth in me, though he were dead, yet shall he live.' "

Simon moved restlessly in his chair, sweeping his hand across his brow in his impatient manner. He was off his guard. He leaned forward; his dark eyes seemed to search Hamish's face with a wild hopelessness.

"How do you *know* that those words are true?" he said, mechanically, as though repeating something he had learned by heart.

There was silence in the room for several seconds and through the open window came the continuous cry of the lambs on the hillside.

Hamish rose suddenly to his feet and with an intensity of emotion surging beneath an exterior which he vainly attempted to keep calm, he said: "Because it is the word of God."

Simon gazed at him meditatively for a moment, then he rose from his chair and went over to the window. How strange was the obscurity of Hamish's mind on the subject of God, he thought. On all other points his intellect was startling in its eager activity, but on this, the subject of supreme interest, intellect had failed, unable to stand up against the enormous unfaceable reality of life and death. Intellect had given place to the intangible flame of faith. Was it blindness or clearness of sight?

Simon sighed heavily; what could it be like to possess a mind unassailed by doubt? He drew his hand across his eyes again and returned slowly to the hearth. After an awkward pause, conversation flowed on, but there was a sudden barrier which had not been there before. They were strangers and alone again.

Hamish, suspicious, that vague fear which lurked at the bottom of his mind stirring once more; the fear that came to him in the dreariest hour of the night sometimes and whispered to him of man's transient and infinitesimal strength and of the grinding, soulless power of time and the relentless mocking of the earth at the piteous atoms that crept over her surface, flattering themselves with dreams.

Simon was wearied; it was always this way— for a moment friendship and kinship with another and then once more the loneliness of plodding on alone, looking at life through eyes that no one could share, a lonely human soul, the most mysterious of all things, coming and going who knows how?

Suddenly born in an uncountable moment, and then dying with all its store of "one-ness" never to be known again.

The following day Hamish was away all day. He was up at the farm which formed part of the property belonging to the Manse. The men were cutting the rushes down by the Cairnach burn to serve as thatch for the farm buildings.

It was a blazing day. The bay lay like glass; the dark hills of the Islands and the great phalanx of white clouds were mirrored in its depth with brilliant clearness; out where the sound narrowed into the kyle the water stirred in oily ripples where the tide was beginning to run.

Allison sat in the Manse parlor, the brilliant light from the window streaming down upon her uplifted face. In the other corner of the room Simon stood before a canvas upon which fell the light from the other window. His eyes were half shut, and he walked uneasily to and fro. Out of courtesy to his host and hostess, he had suggested painting their portraits. The one of Hamish was almost completed. The likeness was good, but Simon was not contented with it. Why was it that execution always fell so far short of conception? He had caught the set of the firm, well-cut mouth, and the arrogant tilt of the massive chin, but the eyes looked out from the picture like two circles of gray glass; they were blobs of paint completing the pattern and symmetry of the face, not the transparent gleaming gateway through which a glimpse of the mind which lay behind could be caught. He was determined that the portrait of Allison should be better.

He had only just begun on it; the head and shoulders were outlined in charcoal, and he was engaged in the laying on of the flat planes of color. Allison sat before him primly, her hands folded in her lap. She wore a stiff black dress of silk, gathered tightly in at the waist; this accentuated the swelling curve of her bosom. A wide lace collar or fichu was pinned decorously up to the throat. The lace was delicate and Allison prized it greatly; she had possessed it before her marriage, when she had frequented the refined middle class circles in a small Highland town.

Her dark brown hair was smoothed back, so that almost all the curl in it was vanquished. Her round, almost childish face, seemed at odds with this stiff attire; her deep reddish brown eyes looked out of the window with the innocent searching expression which was characteristic of them.

Simon talked ceaselessly; sometimes leaving a sentence unfinished, as he caught some par-

ticular shade or form with the swift dashes of
his brush. Allison could see the road from
where she sat, and a glimpse of Ben Buie framed
in the trees that surrounded the Manse. On
the wall opposite to her the shadow of their
leaves made a quivering pattern.

She would dream away her time gazing into
the heat-misted distance, listening absently to
the husky drone of Simon's voice; she felt pleasantly indolent, in a trance from which she had
no desire to rally herself.

She spent a good deal of time thinking of the
children, and of Hamish, and then she found
herself wondering about Andrew Simon himself.

She cast a furtive glance towards him as he
stooped his dark untidy head over his palette.
He was mixing some paint, but his gaze was on
her, ardent and searching.

Something stirred within her for a moment
and the blood mounted to her cheeks. She was
annoyed with herself. Simon often sat gazing
at her like that when he was painting, gaging
the particular depth of some color, or steeping himself in the general atmosphere of his
picture.

There seemed to be something different in

his expression now. A moment later he spoke and she knew she had been right, for usually after he had gazed at her in rapt silence, he would set to work vigorously on his canvas, scratching out with his palette knife, or applying new colors.

He threw down his brush and pushed back his chair. "It seems almost sinful to sit here when it's vastly more beautiful outside," he said, smiling up at her. "Shall we go out? Will you come up to the shoulder of Ben Buie and look over the sea? It's an easy climb and the burn is so low that you needn't fear the water."

Allison had often walked with him before. She enjoyed his conversation. He spoke of things of which she knew nothing; he spoke to her as an equal and took it for granted that she followed his train of thought quite adequately; he never explained to her as Hamish did, and sometimes he left her stumbling far behind, vainly clutching at the outskirts of his meaning.

"I shall have to change my gown," she said, holding out the folds of her black silk with a grace which was natural to her, and had a childishness about it which accorded ill with the sedateness of a minister's wife. He smiled at her again. She looked so bright and childish standing in the light of the window, that Simon sighed involuntarily; the rest of the room was shadowed and gloomy, with its ministerial furniture, the hard-seated chairs and the heavy clock on the mantelpiece. She was very different from the women with whom he had associated, the women of the Regency.

She hurried away to change her frock, laying it away carefully in the chest that held Hamish's best "blacks," which he wore when he visited the towns to help with the Communions, and when he sat in the Presbytery of Loch Norra.

She felt a wildness surging through her, and her recent acquiescence seemed to have disappeared; she would not stop to think a moment. She scrambled into her old gray gown. She almost ran across the landing; the door that led into the nursery stood open. Bella now acted as Nanny to the children, her work in the kitchen having been handed over to two natives of the place whom Hamish wished to employ.

Bella, in her spotless print, was seated in the window sewing. Jean ran forward at the sight of her mother, imploring to be taken out as well.

"But, my wee," said Allison, regarding Bella

nervously, "I'm walking away up the Ben, miles and miles, and it is too hot."

The little girl assured her mother, with round eager eyes, that she could walk any distance; she reminded her of other feats of endurance which she had performed. There was a feeling of fear at the bottom of Allison's heart, something that quaked and beat; the warm pressure of the child that clung so eagerly round her knees reassured her. She assented quickly and Bella, with a few muttered ejaculations as to the heat, fetched Jean's little bonnet and despatched her down the stairs after her mother. Simon was waiting in the sunlight outside the front door.

"You know," he said suddenly as they crossed the yard at the back of the house and entered upon the rock-strewn path that led up the left bank of the burn, "I wish I had painted you as you are now. I always hated the stiff black."

Allison looked up at him disturbed; she secretly admired herself in the black silk, and had hoped that Simon shared her view.

He laughed when he saw the consternation on her face. "I only meant," he said, "that I'd rather have you as yourself than as, well—the minister's wife."

Allison did not know whether to be shocked or pleased at this.

"It's a grand thing to be a minister's wife," she said, uncertainly. "I'd like my grandchildren to see me in my black silk as a minister's wife."

"Your grandchildren!" he exclaimed, with a shout of laughter. "Why, how monstrously entertaining that sounds! You're more fit to be some one's grandchild than to have any yourself!"

"I may be now," she said, smiling, "but when Jean grows up and marries, then her children will look at the portrait and see me in my black silk and think that I look like a minister's wife and then they will respect me."

He looked down on her with a whimsical smile. He knew that she struggled to attain to a dignity which would please Hamish; he had often seen her lips quiver under a note of disapproval in his voice when he upbraided her for behaving "as though she were still a child in her father's house," where he had first met her in her sixteenth year.

"How would it be if your grandchildren were to look at your portrait, and instead of finding what they expected, they found something quite different—supposing they found something young and beautiful and joyful—supposing they saw in the portrait the picture that I am looking at now?"

Andrew Simon did not mean to make love to her in his husky, eager voice, for his reverence for her innocence and beauty of spirit had grown with the month which he had spent in her company. But it was second nature to him to please a pretty woman, and he had the knack of words and his emotions were easily stirred.

Allison looked up at him again, the blood mounting to her cheeks. He was walking so fast, in spite of his limp, and she was panting a little.

Jean flew in front of them like a little animal, her bonnet halfway down her back, and her fair curls standing out in disorder all over her head. The path grew steeper and steeper, so that conversation was restricted; the heat was really very great. The child began to lag behind, until Simon picked her up and carried her on his shoulders. Very soon he stopped in the shade of a rowan tree that swung its branches invitingly over the path. He threw himself down in the heather, panting and wip-

ing the sweat from his eyes with the back of
his hand.

Allison seated herself carefully and demurely
on a crotal-covered rock near by. The child
sat in the heather, leaning against her knee; the
restless gray eyes were closing and the little head
nodded, and gradually sank forward in sleep.

Simon lay flat on his back with his knees
crooked upwards. His eyes were closed and
the light of the sun through the lids was transformed into a rose-colored haze.

"If I walk very fast," he said, "this disagree-
able leg of mine begins to let me know of its
existence."

The sunlight on his face accentuated the
lines, deep-cut round his eyes and at the corners of his mouth.

"You know, I've often wondered," replied
Allison, "how it was that you damaged your leg
and your hand, but I—well, I didn't think that
perhaps I ought to ask you." She wished he
would rise from his unconventional position
and open his eyes.

"Why not?" inquired Simon, with that dis-
concerting suddenness that always took away
her breath. "Are you afraid of me?" he con-

tinued, and then as she did not answer, he said:
"Very well, Madam, I'll tell you."

There was a pause and the crying of the
lambs on the solitary hillside became more insistent.

"I had a ball lodged in my knee, and a saber-
cut on my hand at Waterloo," he began, his
voice even more husky than usual. "It was
seventeen years ago—I was eighteen at the time.
I sometimes think that there was more in that
ball than mere lead. They talk about the iron
entering into a man's soul." He laughed grimly
and continued more seriously, "After Waterloo
a sort of bitterness came over me which has
never left me since. Sometimes I am free from
it for months at a time, and then it comes sweeping down on me and I am helpless again." His
voice was drowsier now, and it seemed to Allison as though he spoke to himself. "I had
fought at Quatre Bras two days before, and the
previous day we were marching most of the
time. I was so tired on the morning of
the eighteenth that everything seemed rather insignificant and pointless. I did not feel elevated
or noble; I was not even excited as I had been
at Quatre Bras. We stood and waited; our lot
were holding the farm and orchard of Hougou-

mont; we were detached from the main forces
hidden by the shoulder of the hill. I could
have laughed to think that perhaps I was standing just outside death. I said to myself now I
shall *know* what happens, whether a man's
spirit is immortal or mere dust to dust."

He had more or less forgotten Allison now.
She was startled by his words, and the bitterness of his tone, but before she could speak
he went on again.

"That scene as it lay before me made an im-
pression which will never fade from my mind;
I suppose my sensibilities were sharpened, although I was unaware of it." He smiled at her.
"It was all so green and orderly; before the battle there were cornfields and clover-fields—you
know, the corn was only half grown. There
had been much rain and I never smell the rich
damp smell of spring without thinking of those
fields, a faint haze rising from them. The Brussels road cut like a dead white ribbon through
the fields; we could see the walls of La Haye
Sainte gleaming in the sun, too."

His voice grew drowsy and he paused; then
he went on again slower and more painfully.
"The attack did not come till about eleven;
I was in tne orchard and the petals of some

late fruit trees were scattered all over my arm, as I lay behind a broken-down wall holding my musket. The French had been very quiet, but the air seemed charged with a tremulous suspense; and then they came. At first the short distance between us seemed impassable somehow, and then the cornfields and the sunlight and the blossoms disappeared, and there was nothing but thundering horses, and blood, and the smell of powder, and there was a man screaming on the other side of the orchard, and the rattle of grape-shot and dull crash of cannon-balls. Much later, I suppose it must have been about three o'clock, when I was lying there face downwards in the mud—I can remember now how it oozed through my fingers when I dug them into the ground—and two of the fingers weren't there—I suddenly thought for the first time, why all this bloodshed, this terrible suffering? Why, if God is all-merciful, is such cruelty and suffering permitted? I did not care; I wanted to die. And four hours later, when I had lain in the mud and the sun until I was light-headed, I laughed when I heard them shouting and cheering. The orchard was full of men huddled in strange attitudes, and horses—" He stopped suddenly. "If you could have seen the horses—"

Despair had crept into his voice. He went on more quietly, "I was sent home to my father's house in Renfrewshire and there I remained until the bitterness became unbearable. Whilst I sat at a table eating with silver spoons and forks, unable to taste half of what was set before me, because of its superabundance, there were miners in the district round, who were starving, to whom the value of one of the forks with which I ate would have supplied food and fuel for several days. When the miserable starving wretches rebelled, they were told lies and sent away trustful, and nothing was done for them. They were oppressed and there was no one to lead them or lift them up; when the black fit was on me I would go away to some solitary place and attempt to comfort myself by painting and by living with the sea and hills only around me, or I would rush into all the excitement and folly of London. But there is no comfort. I look for it no longer—happiness, pure happiness and comfort, are figments of the brain, just as were the Atlantis and Utopia. The men in the cities still starved whether I walked the hills, gambled in St. James's Street, or sat at my father's table."

He sighed restlessly, and, opening his eyes, he seemed aware of her presence once more. Her face was flushed and her hands clasped in her lap. She leaned towards him and said, shyly: "There is comfort in the Lord. The Minister says—" She stopped at the look on his face; her voice was rather uncertain. She rubbed her fingers up and down on her knee nervously.

Simon sat up suddenly and with the blunt cruelty of which he was sometimes guilty, he said: "What kind of comfort have you ever got from the Lord? Whatever comfort exists comes from man's own brain; insomuch as man is God himself, then comfort comes from the Lord. What if the Lord were a convenient figment like so many other objects of the fetish worship of human existence?"

Allison could feel her heart thumping in her breast. The heat was terrific. What was Simon saying? She ought not to listen. He was a man of sin; she must tell Hamish at once what he had said. She must not stay a moment longer in his presence. Yet she still sat rooted to the rock, a great pity for him surging across her brain. She raised her eyes to meet his; the suffering in them was like a knife-thrust to her; she seemed to see through into the dark terrors of his mind. Thus, when he stretched out his hand and laid it on her knee, she did not move. There was silence. She dared not speak lest the trembling of her voice should betray her agitation. He saw the consternation in her face, and the quick tears which had risen to her eyes.

"I am sorry," he said simply. "I should not have said what I have said—forgive me—I forgot myself; I don't know why—perhaps because I was afraid of my loneliness."

She smiled at him and spoke. "There is nothing to forgive, Mr. Simon; it is only pity for you that makes me weep."

She wiped away her tears with her small handkerchief. He rose to his feet and lifting her hand to his lips, kissed it with that odd courtesy that seldom forsook him.

"Shall we go on," he said quietly, "or would you rather go back to the Manse?"

Allison was making an effort to calm herself. Why was she so disturbed by his words? "Shall we go up to the top?" she said quietly.

He held out his hand to the small Jean, who

stood rubbing her eyes with her fists. All the
way up the twisting path he chattered to the
child. They came at last to the place where
they must cross the burn. The water was so
low that there was no difficulty, although in the
winter there had been a rushing volume of
amber, foam-flecked water thundering between
the rocks. As Simon stretched out his maimed
hand to assist her across the shifting stones, she
thought again of his bitterness with a pity and
a horror that she could not understand; but
now he was laughing, his hazel eyes were alight,
he had thrust a piece of early heather behind
his ear, he looked like an eager boy, all the
hard lines that she had seen in his face, ten
minutes earlier, seemed smoothed away. He
scrambled up the opposite bank on all fours,
Jean shouting for joy at his heels. All the
way up the path on the opposite brae he chattered on. He was telling the child a story; she
held his hand and gazed up into his face, as
though she must, at all costs, see the movement
of his lips to understand his words.

"And the big white stone rolled and rolled
down from the burn into the farmyard behind
the Manse, and it rolled into the kitchen, and
it rolled into the parlor, and it rolled against

the swing door of the study where Papa was writing his sermon, and then it rolled right in and Papa said: 'Do you know the Catechism and all the names of the Books in the Bible?' "

"But why did Papa ask a stone?" inquired Jean, breathlessly.

"He thought that the stone was his little girl, Jean, because he had never looked up, as he was so busy writing his sermon."

"And then where did the stone roll?" interrupted the child, hanging all her small weight on his arm.

"It rolled down the hill to the sea and then —it splashed and splashed, and sank right to the bottom, and all the fishermen thought it was a whale that they had heard, and they put out into the kyle in their boats with nets."

"But it was just the old stone," assisted Jean.

"Yes, it was the old stone, and at the bottom of the sea there was a beautiful cave of coral and green seaweed."

"And lobsters and frogs and poor dead seagulls come alive again, and angels and dogfishes," supplemented Jean, giving free rein to her imagination. "And the Egyptians all tied up in stringy seaweed?"

Simon glanced down at Allison, who had

caught them up; his eyes danced with amusement. She was not sure whether the Catechism should be introduced into a mythological story, or whether her daughter should be permitted to mention angels and the Egyptians in the same breath with frogs and lobsters, as dwellers beneath the sea; but as soon as Simon went on describing the bottom of the sea, she was carried away by his eloquence, her interest was almost as great as that of the child.

Then suddenly they came over the brow of the hill and looked southward over the sea and the hills of Knoydart. The mountains stood like mountains in cloud-land, ethereal, intangible, as though they would melt into mist and distance. A haze hung over the sea, and far away the Island of Loga lay on the horizon like the fin of a giant fish. Closer in, the water glittered with a transparent silver. In the distance to the right, the shattered peaks of the Coolins cut into the sky, blue and splintered. The sky was cloudless and transparent, an arch of eternity.

Simon stopped in the middle of his narration and gazed out in silence over the scene.

Jean persisted with her questions. "But

what happened to the big white stone when it escaped from the cave?"

"Hush, my wee," whispered Allison, laying her hand softly over the child's mouth.

"Why did you say that?" queried Simon suddenly.

She had not thought that he was listening, so rapt had been his expression. "You seemed so —so happy," she said, awkwardly, "I did not want her to disturb you."

"I was happy," he said quickly. "I am happy now." He drew in his breath sharply, stretching out his fingers. "Do you know what the poet Keats used to say: 'Oh, for a life of sensations rather than of thought'—that's what I often pray for."

"But the thoughts always seem to come," said Allison gravely. "I often pretend things aren't real; but sooner or later I find they are, and no amount of dreaming or inventing can make them less real—when they're real they've got to be faced and understood."

She wondered to herself why she was saying this; she had never voiced this opinion before, but then she had so many ideas in her head that had never gone any further. So many of them seemed to be coming to life in the course of her conversations with Simon.

"That is true enough," Simon replied rather sadly. "Reality is one of the things which I know is not to be surmounted, yet I attempt to do so over and over again—and live in a fool's paradise."

They sat in silence for a minute or two. The air was very still and they could hear the cry of the seagulls far below in the bay. Presently Allison rose to go. Hamish would be returning soon. He would be tired and might want her to read to him or rub his aching limbs.

Something stirred within her at the thought that he still needed her. She hurried down the steep path. Simon helped her over the dyke as though she were the Queen of England, turning his head discreetly away as she stepped upwards. Offering her his arm he led her into the house. He said nothing, but as they parted in the hall, he darted a quick look at her and his face broke into a sudden smile.

She hurried up the stairs. What kind of man was this who first lay heartbroken, the futility of the world grinding him down so that nothing was left; who spoke terrible blasphemies, for so she thought them; and then stood smiling at her like a boy and telling her she was a pretty woman.

She heard the sound of Hamish's voice in the hall and she hurried down to meet him. He kissed her absently. His skin was burnt to a dull red, his gray eyes blazed with health and eagerness. She hurried to the kitchen to tell the maids to take fresh water to his room.

Chapter X

THAT night, after his long day's labor, Hamish fell asleep in his leather chair. His strong, well-shaped hands lay along the worn green arms; the blue veins stood out in a gnarled tracing; the gold signet-ring on the small finger of his left hand caught the light of the fire and glinted.

Hamish was tired physically, but his mind had been filled with a new vigor. While he had stooped over the rushes, swinging his scythe with a never-ceasing rhythm, his eager mentality had been ranging from one thing to another like a wild animal that sniffs at what it finds and turns it over before devouring it or hiding it away for future use. He had pondered mostly on the incomprehensible cruelty of human nature—the fierce unreasonableness of everything. Men were denied their rights, trodden down by those of a meaner spirit than themselves, because of greed and fear. What, after all, were land and money?

"Lay up for yourself treasure in heaven."

Even here in the remote glen, cut off from the rest of the world for half the year by snow and mist, sheep owners of larger sheep farms were always attempting to thrust out the small individual farmers, who labored diligently on their few stony acres with their sheep.

When at last the smaller farmers gave in and sold their land, there was nothing left for them; they must either live on, poverty-stricken, in a world of dreams, often full of an anguish that could only be drowned in the hot raw whisky, or else the unflinching spirit in some of these small individual farmers must seek freedom in Canada or Australia.

Only that morning Donald McAllister, the young fisherman who had helped him to land his furniture, had come to Hamish; the usual quiet atmosphere that surrounded him was stirred, a glow burnt deep in his gray eyes.

"I can stand out no longer," he said, in his slow quiet English, translating from the Gaelic in his own mind as he spoke. "They are all turned against me. Grierson up at Invermorarty needs my two fields to add to his acres and no man dares to help me; for where are they to get their extra potatoes in the winter —and the potatoes look very bad indeed; if they anger Grierson of Invermorarty, they may starve in the winter. I have no plow. The calf has died and the cow seems likely to go along the same road; I have no money to buy good food for her. My sheep are worth nothing to me without the land." He spoke impersonally, as though relating the misfortunes of another.

"I would go with the boat that takes them away to Canada," he continued slowly, "but there is the wife and the young one—but when the weather becomes rough and there's no more warmth from the sea—I think we will go. Starvation is a terrible thing."

Hamish had gone to see the cow, which lay in a miserable shed on some fresh-cut rushes. Donald spoke to her in Gaelic, crooning softly as though he were speaking to a child. The beast lifted its head slowly, and gazed at him with its huge liquid eyes; the saliva hung from the corners of its pale mouth. As soon as he rose, it laid its head down crookedly on the rushes again. There were tears in Donald's fierce eyes as he rose, and the harsh lines of his dark face seemed to be crumpled.

"It is the evil-eye they have put on her," he said in Gaelic.

Hamish was appalled. Donald had been one of the few regular attendants at the kirk, and yet even he could speak of the evil-eye with a sullen finality.

" 'Tis the old wife from the cairn-side that they have put on to gaze upon the poor harmless beast—and so her calf died and now she pines away with a broken heart." He caressed the cow's ear with huge, gentle fingers.

Hamish had remonstrated, but he saw that the man was not convinced at all.

"There are the things we know," he said, slowly, "and there are many things we do not."

Outside the sun had blazed on the grass and everything was moving inevitably towards ripeness and fruition.

As Hamish had slashed at the rushes he had gloried in the strength of his own body; he liked the sight of his own forearm, the muscles strained, as it swung backwards and forwards, the sweat gleaming on it. At first, as he worked he had been filled with a dark fear: the odds against him seemed too great. Men must be free, must realize their own greatness of spirit, but how could this ever be, when human nature, oppressed for generations, fumbled in darkness and superstition, turning hither and thither in blind bewilderment? What though they should learn to see truth in time to come? There would always be those below who struggled in darkness—what if those who had climbed upwards towards the light of freedom should grind down those below them?

Gradually the sun and the clear sudden breeze which came up off the sea entered into his mind and he rejoiced in his health and strength; hope began to rise in him again, and he worked so that the sweat ran down into his eyes; the pure flame of faith burnt within him once more.

As he lay asleep in his chair, something of this happiness lingered in his face. Simon, sitting opposite, idly turning over Johnson's "Journey to the Western Isles," which Hamish had given him, glanced at him often. Why was it that through all the overwhelming adversity which assailed a man, this Highland minister could sleep with an expression of glorying thankfulness upon his face?

Before he had fallen asleep he had been talking angrily of the Catholic Emancipation Bill, which had been passed some four years earlier. That a man of Sir Robert Peel's intellect could allow such a thing, having fought and beaten

Canning on the very same ground, was beyond
Hamish's comprehension. Sir Robert Peel,
backed by the hero of the nation, the Duke,
had allowed Papists responsibility in govern-
ing the British Nation!

At first Simon had smiled inwardly at the
narrow bigotry of the Scots minister; he spoke
of the "Papists" as though they were rabid dogs
or criminal lunatics, to be locked up or ex-
terminated; then suddenly he saw that there
was more than the petty hatred of sect for sect
which existed so strongly at that time, and was
to grow stronger in the coming years. There
was at the bottom of his hatred a consciousness
of man's divine spirit and a love of freedom,
which glowed through all his actions and made
life one long struggle for him, but not a weary
struggle without hope. Men were evil, they
had lost all sense of original blessedness, but
still far down in their spirits burned the fire of
God; fan this flame, reveal it to mankind, and
freedom would burst forth like some perfect
pure flood of light.

"A man who is a Catholic," Hamish said,
"barters away the freedom of his spirit, the Divine Spirit which comes straight from the Lord,
the Giver. There can be no intermediary

between the man and God, no intercessor."

Simon had pondered; how much of this hatred was pure bigotry? How much was a deep-rooted aversion which had grown up in Covenanting Scotland? That there was a genuine faith in freedom he did not doubt; he had never known a man of such an unstained and steady faith in the spirit of God.

Hamish had condemned the bewilderment of people that could not face the mysteries of religion and fled for certainty to the Roman Catholic Church; yet, Simon wondered, did he, Hamish, face them himself; did any one? What was immortality but a comforting sop that man had offered himself through the ages, ever since he had grown conscious of the complete cessation of the individual with death? What was God Himself but a pleasing and glorified image of man himself, adopting man's standards of right and wrong? Men had invented these standards to delude themselves into the belief that life was great and glorious and important. Yet he found it impossible to believe nothing. When he had recovered from his wounds after the war, he had moped in his father's house in Renfrewshire, brooding on the injustice and

fruitlessness of the world. Cynicism descended
upon him like a blight, withering all his youthful enthusiasms. In this mood he was sent to
London to enter society with a view to Parliament.

He threw himself recklessly into the im-
morality and the squandering of money which
was characteristic of the London of the day.
He did all that the fashionable did. He danced
at Almack's clad in breeches and silk stockings; he went to the Opera; he played for
enormous stakes in St. James's Street. He
knew all the beautiful women of the day, being
particularly attentive to three charming grand-
daughters of Sheridan. He knew the shunned
Lady Blessington intimately, and her dandy,
impoverished son-in-law, the Count d'Orsay.
He kept a mistress, as all smart young men
about town did; but as he had told Allison
that afternoon on the side of Ben Buie the
zest had gone out of things—he seemed to be
skimming over the black depths of a slough.

Until 1825, he had lived this scarlet-and-gold
existence like a dead man: popular with men
as a rich and reckless scamp, and loved by many
women. Then quite suddenly he had thrown
up all Parliamentary ambitions and fled to

Paris, where he painted spasmodically for five
years, seeing no one, hearing no news of England, attempting to forget the horrors of a tinsel
world, steeping himself in debauchery.

For two years he had been back now, and the
old sadness seemed to have dropped from him.
He attempted to live in the happiness of the
present moment; he would entangle himself
with human affairs no longer, nor with human
institutions.   It was only occasionally that his
sensations betrayed him, and he found himself
in the slough of thought once again.

Since he had been in this Highland Manse,
he had been made to think too much.   Hamish
was so insistent with his questions about the
conditions in the Renfrewshire coal mines, or
the corrupt electorate system, or the patronage
of clergy, or, in fact, of anything.   Then in
June had come the Reform Bill to stimulate
discussion.

Yes, he must go away as soon as the portrait
of Allison was finished, or life might become
unbearable for him once again.

He glanced once more at Hamish's peaceful
face.   What could he know of Freedom in this
out-of-the-world parish, of mankind trodden
down and brutalized?   He was nothing but a

visionary. Simon sneered unhappily to himself.

At nine o'clock Allison came in bearing the
tray with the tea in its locked caddy upon it.
She had seen that the sugar had been cut into
reasonable-sized lumps, and not served in
broken pieces.

When tea had been drunk, Allison, standing on tiptoe, reached the heavy Bible from its
shelf and took it to Hamish.

"You read to-night, my dear," he said sleepily. "I am tired with the strong air, and my
throat is dry with the dust."

Allison composed herself opposite to her husband, the heavy book resting on her knees; she
tried to persuade herself that she was not
nervous. She had often read to Hamish before;
he had told her that her elocution was good
and her voice pleasant. There was no need to
fear; but still, her heart thudded against her
ribs. She could feel Simon's intent gaze upon
her.

"What shall I read?" she inquired, very low,
her eyes still on the pages, her nervous fingers
fluttering them over unconsciously.

"Read the Hundred-and-second Psalm," said

Hamish absently, his thoughts for the moment elsewhere.

Allison looked very demure in her soft gray frock, the light from the lamp falling on her dark hair, her little feet on the toes, just peeping from beneath her voluminous skirt. There was a flush on her cheeks and her bosom rose and fell hurriedly. She read in her gentle child-like voice.

Simon listened more attentively than Hamish, as one who is new to a time-honored custom which has become monotonous to others, may watch proceedings with all eagerness.

" 'For my days are consumed like smoke and my bones are burned as an hearth . . . I am like a pelican of the wilderness, I am like an owl of the desert. I watch and am as a sparrow alone upon the house-top . . . My days are like a shadow that declineth and I am withered like grass.' "

When she had finished reading, she bade them good night, curtsying shyly to Simon. When she had gone he strolled out into the soft dusk of the Highland night.

A sudden sadness seemed to envelop him; the words of the Psalm lingered in his head. "My days are like a shadow that declineth, and I am withered like grass."

He strolled down the twisted ribbon road towards the sea; it was faintly discernible in the transparency of the dusk. The dew had fallen, drenching the grass at the roadside. There was a faint breeze which came in gusts from the sea, the smell of salt-soaked seaweed was wafted with it. When he reached the tumbled-down gray dyke which separated the road from the shore, he sat down and filled his clumsy pipe, awkwardly because of his injured fingers. The sea lapped on the stones with a muffled sound; every now and again the backwash made a louder incomprehensible rush, and then settled into the continuous lapping again. The sky was delicate and fairylike, and seemed like dark blue gauze drawn over a space of light insufferable. There was no moon. A boat passed, hidden by the semi-darkness, but the creak of the rowlocks and the splash of the oars came to his ears with startling clearness. Across the sound he could see the mountains of the Islands dimly silhouetted; a light twinkled on the northern headland. He could not think, he only sat there feeling the loveliness of the earth.

A fire burned on the green before the crofts farther along the shore. It blazed brightly, wavering very slightly in the soft breeze. After a while he rose quietly, walking in the soft drenched grass at the roadside lest he should break the tranced silence. Slowly he climbed the road towards the Manse. He thought of Hamish, sleeping in the green leather chair, a smile of triumph and glory on his lips. He raised his eyes to the vast slopes of Ben Buie, and his ears were filled with the sound of the water falling into the linn on the mountainside. Suddenly the wind came tearing down the glen, stirring the trees round the Manse into agitation. Simon shuddered at the pitiableness of human existence.

The drive was very dark, and the heavy dew on the moss made it slippery. He hurried forward, his uneven, limping footsteps thudding through the damp air. Suddenly he missed his footing and came down heavily among the rotting leaves at the side of the drive.

For a moment he lay slightly stunned. His ankle had doubled beneath him. When he attempted to move, a hot pain shot up his leg. A blackness fringed with odd colored lights came before his eyes; he swore softly to himself.

Presently he raised himself with difficulty, and, half crawling, half hopping, he arrived at length at the side door of the Manse, which was often left unlocked. There were no lights to be seen in the house.

He crept painfully up to his bedroom, and flinging off his coat and trousers, climbed into bed. His ankle throbbed, and fierce hot pains shot up his leg, yet he was shivering. Pain was insufferable to him; the wounds from which he had suffered had left a double scar; his over-sensitive nerves seemed on fire. He rose once and plunged the swollen foot into a jug of ice-cold water.

Presently he could bear it no longer. He staggered down the stairs again as quietly as he was able—perhaps there might be boiling water in the kitchen. The fire was still alight as he supported himself into the cold stone-flagged room; there was water in an iron pot on the side, but it was scarcely more than tepid. He dropped the poker twice upon the flags. His candle needed snuffing; in his endeavor to effect this delicate operation with his fingers, he extinguished it altogether; in vain he struggled to light it by thrusting it through the bars of the grate. The candle melted away but failed to light.

Suddenly there was a light in the doorway and Hamish's voice rang out harsh and loud in the stillness.

"Who is there?"

"It's only I, Simon," replied the exasperated Simon in his low husky voice. "I slipped and hurt my ankle when I was out and I couldn't sleep—I came to see if there was any hot water to bathe it with. I apologize if I have disturbed you." His voice was cold.

Hamish was angry. Allison had awakened him from a sound sleep. She had been trembling with fright. At first he had refused to stir from the warmth of his bed, but when the sound of the dropped poker resounded through the house, he had issued forth.

"There will be no hot water here," he said coldly; "the fire is almost out. I should advise resting your foot in bed."

Simon stood silent. Rage rose up in his soul; he felt ill-used and misunderstood; his ankle was sending fierce shoots of pain up his leg. Without a word he limped past Hamish, along the passage and up the stairs. He had walked

on all fours before, but this he did not deign to
do before such utter sarcasm; it would have
spoiled the idea of his own nobility which was
forming in his mind.

By the time he reached the top of the stairs,
all thoughts of nobility had vanished, he strove
only to keep upright; darkness and green and
purple lights alternated before his eyes.   He
entered his room and sank down upon the bed,
sick with pain.

Hamish found Allison just behind the door.
She was wrapped in a thick padded dressing-
gown of his; her eyes were round with excitement and fear.   She plied him with rapid
questions.   The mantle of sleep, however, had
descended upon him once more as he clambered
into bed; he would do no more than mutter
about a fall, a hurt ankle and hot water.

Allison was bewildered.   She had watched
Simon through a chink in the door.   She had
stood on the landing until he had begun to
ascend the stairs, when, filled with panic by her
boldness, she had returned behind the door.
The vision of his pale, nerve-racked face
troubled her gentle heart.   She glanced towards
the bed.   Nothing was to be seen of Hamish
save the tip of his night-cap.

She crept out onto the landing. There was absolute silence save for the heavy ticking of the clock in the hall beneath, which seemed to vary in its rhythm as she listened. She moved silently over to his door—there was no movement; then she caught the sound of a heavy sigh and a suppressed groan as he turned over in bed.

She returned hurriedly to her room. Hamish's breathing was regular and powerful; he was asleep once more. She selected some cooling ointment and a linen bandage from her medicine chest, then she hurried onto the landing once more.

Her spirits misgave her. What would Hamish say? Could she possibly enter a man's room alone and in her night attire? In spite of the fact that she had enveloped herself in a dressing-gown and hidden her hair under a lace mob-cap, she felt indecently clad. The blood mounted to her cheeks. She began to shiver as she waited outside the door; then she heard him groan again, and involuntarily she raised her hand and knocked. When the deed was done, fear and remorse overcame her and she wished to fly. She heard his husky, "Come in." She opened the door and went inside.

The room was in great disorder; his jacket lay in one corner and his trousers in another; his shoes were in the middle of the room and the ewer of water stood beside his bed. The candle guttered in the draught; the window was wide open and the curtains ballooned into the room as she entered.

The bed was in no better plight; the clothes were half on the floor, the pillows were lumped into uncomfortable masses.

He raised his tousled dark head as she entered. He was surprised to see her, but relieved; the sight of her standing there filled him with confidence, she would know what to do with his confounded foot.

"I've brought you some cooling ointment for your foot, Mr. Simon," she faltered, advancing and laying it on the table at his bedside. She longed to stay and bind up the swollen foot, which lay outside the coverlet, but she dared not. It was not fear of Hamish's waking that checked her, but a nebulous, indefinable fear which she did not understand.

Simon thanked her with a wry smile. Even though his foot was paining him considerably, he did not fail to take in the picture of Allison standing there, with a candle in her hand, her dark hair escaping from her cap. He looked at her fixedly, his hazel eyes very bright beneath his tousled hair.

It was a long time since he had looked at a woman who inspired him with reverence: Allison's innocence and gentleness seemed almost incredible to him; it was so long since he had associated at all intimately with women of this kind, that he had almost forgotten that they existed. At the same time she was very desirable, with her beautiful brown eyes and pretty hands and wrists.

With a hurried "good night" Allison fled from the room. She turned the handle softly as she entered her own room. Hamish still slept. She crept into her bed beside him and lay for some time staring into the darkness; she did not want to think, but a strong consciousness of an impending excitement disturbed her.

Chapter XI

And so the time drew near for Hamish's journey to Edinburgh to assist in the administration of the Sacrament in a parish there. He was to stay with another minister to whom he had promised his help several months before. Other plans had been maturing in his head also. There was much that his parish needed. The church itself was eaten away by the salted damp of the sea; there was a mere pittance of relief in the Poor Fund which he had organized with such care and labor. Should the potato crop fail, which seemed more than likely, what would become of the people—wretched starving outcasts that they were, driven this way and that by their landlords and the larger farmers. Year after year, what was left of them went away to seek new life in Canada or Australia. The old ones were sometimes left behind because there was no passage money. Sometimes young men would fail to gather the requisite sum, small as it was, and they would remain in the glen, until the mist and the raw wild spirit of the whisky sank into their very souls and there was nothing left of real men but a far-away elusive expression in their eyes.

Thoughts of London had always fired Hamish's imagination; the hub of the nation, where great statesmen sat and debated with one another under the shadow of the Houses of Parliament. It filled him with an uplifting thrill to think of the powers of organization centered there. In the picture he drew himself of London, riches always played a conspicuous part, the flash of rich colors and gold. Since Andrew Simon had been in the glen, these pictures of London had grown upon him, and although he knew of the squalor and miserable poverty, of the disease and filth bordering on the dark evil-smelling lips of the Thames, the vision of brightly lighted streets, men in silk stockings and, above all, money, persisted in his mind.

This picture had an irresistible fascination for him; it was evil, it was the flesh and the devil—and he had never seen it.

Surely, then, it was to London he must go to gather charity for his own starving people. When he had finished with his duties in Edinburgh, he would take ship to Leith, and in the

bright streets of London he would meet those
(he could obtain introductions through members of the Church) whose gold would be nothing to them. He would return with the money
for the people. He would make them work for
it, so that they should not lose their independ-
ence; he had already planned this. There
should be a causeway made from the road
across the shingle in the bay where the ferries
could land safely: thus goods could be drawn
along without danger of losing them in the
transport. The people would have work and
food and warmth, and it would be his doing,
of course with the connivance of the Lord Himself. Uncertainty was beginning to leave Hamish; in days gone by doubt would sway him
cruelly; sometimes he could remember having
been in an agony, not being sure of the Lord's
will.

Now it was different: he felt himself to be
the tool of the Maker, his will was the Lord's,
or rather, as he preferred to express it, the
Lord's will was his.

There was one little grain of doubt, however,
which still disturbed the serenity of his con-
science: his journey would take some time; was
he justified in leaving his parish to the care of

other ministers who would come and preach when they could, or when the weather permitted? Still the fear haunted him which had been borne in upon him so strongly on the night nearly a year ago, when the communicants had drunk and screamed in his own barn; the glint in their eyes had never wholly left him. It was a chance stroke which finally decided him.

Smallpox broke out in the glen; it carried away several children. It spread unrest and fear among the people like some insurrectionist; their nerves were on edge. Owing to the distance which separated the dwellings, the disease did not increase rapidly, but nothing seemed to stamp it out. It would break out again after an interval. It seemed that the glen would never be free from it. The people, already weakened by cholera which had swept Scotland, considered this as another of the necessary evils of life; many of them were pitted with the marks of it. But this year the attacks of the disease were more deadly and more frequent.

Hamish had shaken his head sadly as he saw the talisman hung over the mantelpiece to ward off the plague. He considered it his duty to inform the people of the futility and popishness of this practice, but the talisman did not disappear. Then one day, after he had been working with the sheep up behind the Manse, he was wandering home in the gloaming, the softness of the evening light creeping into the hard crags of his mind; suddenly his eyes filled with tears, because of the helplessness and unutterable pathos of the people attacked by poverty and disease. When he reached home he questioned Simon closely on the subject of injecting lymph from calves to ward off the smallpox. Simon gave him the general idea of the process, although he was not conversant with the details.

Hamish's mind was made up. He would fetch the lymph from London, he would obtain instructions in the administration of it, and return to the glen bringing money and health to the people. It should be the beginning of a new era—also he would see the Houses of Parliament standing above the Thames as he had seen them so often in pictures; one of his long-cherished dreams would be realized.

And then Simon broke his ankle. Only four days remained before Hamish must set off for Edinburgh. The Manse was the home for wandering travelers and people who needed a roof where there was no inn, but he could not leave

Allison alone.   He had never thought of it until the night after Simon had broken his foot.
Allison and he had been sitting in his study in
silence; he was preparing his sermon and she
was idly turning the pages of a book, as she sat
in the chair opposite him.   Suddenly she looked
across at him; then she leaned forward and said
slowly and distinctly:

"Hamish, when you go on Tuesday, shall you
take Mr. Simon with you?"

There had been silence in the room for a second except for the furtive dropping of a scrap
of wood from the grate.

"My dear, he will not be recovered enough,"
he had answered, scarcely glancing up from his
work.   Then he had felt her eyes on him again,
searching, almost beseeching him for something
he did not understand.

"But—but he cannot stay here with no man
in the house," she faltered; there was a strange
metallic ring in her soft voice which arrested
his attention.

"As you will, my dear," he replied.   "I will
see to it to-morrow."

Once more he was immersed in his sermon.
The tragic appeal in Allison's eyes had passed
him by and yet there was relief in her mind;

she had done her part, she had asked that Andrew might go, even if Hamish did not understand; Andrew would go and everything would be well. Then unaccountably she turned her head aside and tears blinded her eyes. She rose, kissed him gently good night and went upstairs. He did not raise his eyes from his sermon.

When Hamish pointed out to Simon that it would be convenient and taken as a favor, if he could make other arrangements whilst Hamish was away, Simon was taken aback, but only because he had never thought of the matter. His dark eyes gleamed with good humor; he arranged to lodge with Donald McAllister in his croft down by the sea. He and Hamish were perfectly satisfied. Allison bowed her head; she was afraid, more afraid than she had ever been before; a weight of foreboding seemed to hang over her. She would not allow herself to think; she brushed Hamish's clothes, she ironed his handkerchiefs, she packed little bottles of homemade cures into the toes of his stockings and boots, so that they might be safe; she packed the boots in a valise which she strapped with her own hands, although the leather was hard from disuse, and the buckles stiff.

The morning upon which Hamish was to depart was cloudy. The sun was there, however, ready to fling its light in a splashing bucketful over the hillsides; as the boat drew into the bay, the sunlight was obscured behind the masses of gray and white clouds, tumbled together in a pile. The seagulls circled round the boat, screaming and screeching and diving angrily for the refuse that floated round her. The wind dashed about the little waiting crowd. Hamish's black cloak swirled out, now straining like a wild thing, now ballooning out comfortably. He clasped his tall black hat with his hand. Willing hands flung his luggage into the rowing boat which was to take him out to the ship. Many of his parishioners, men and women, had come to see him off; they knew his mission was for them and there was a sort of solemnity in the air.

For the first time a forlorn feeling crept into Hamish's soul; for the first time he looked down at Allison hungrily. Her face was flushed by the wind, and strands of dark hair escaped from her bonnet. She was so small that she scarcely reached his shoulder.

The men were shouting from below that the boat was ready. He stooped and kissed Jean, who clung excitedly to her mother's arm, hold-

ing out her tiny shawl in the wind that she
might see the fringe flutter. The bright little
face was lifted to his against the background of
the cold hills plunged in shadow, hills where
mist and cold and disease were waiting for a
few months to pass, before they let loose their
chuckling legions to gather round the glen and
blot it away from the world.

Then he drew Allison to him and kissed her
on the forehead. For a moment she clung to
him and then let him go quite quietly.

"Do not forget the sick woman at Brachan-
tie," he called to her over his shoulder, but
the wind tossed his words away so that she only
caught the echo of "sick woman."

She smiled at him, waving her hand as the
boat drew out from the strand, the rowlocks
creaking, the shock of the water slapping and
shuddering against the bow. Hamish sat in
the stern, gazing outward to the ship. The wake
of the rowing boat was smooth and dotted with
gleaming foam. From the ship waiting in the
sound, the angry flapping of sails and creaking
spars came floating inland in the lull between
the gusts.

Suddenly the sun flung itself from behind the
rolling mass of clouds, its light drenched the

sea and flickered like running water over the hillsides until all was bright save the dark sides of the mountains opposite.

Simon had insisted upon seeing Hamish off. He sat astride a rough sheltie, as his foot was still useless. He and Allison watched the ship gather together like an animal shaking itself, and glide into the wind, which filled the sails gently, and then tore and strained at them in an ecstasy of strength. From shadow to light she darted until she was hidden by the southern headland.

Still the two figures stood motionless, although the people had begun to move off a little time before. The child Jean was straining at her mother's hand, chattering, asking her of "Papa's ship, Papa's journey, Papa's hat."

Simon watched in silence. He had not turned his head away when the husband and wife had parted: he was curious to see how Allison would take the separation from her husband. There was something about her which made him want to make love to her always, but there was something stronger and stranger which filled him with a curious awe. What went on in the brain behind that round childish face, behind those soft brown eyes which filled with tears so easily when pity was stirred in her heart?

She raised her eyes to his with a sigh. Then she came over and stood beside his pony. "Would you take Jean up beside you?" she asked him. "It is rough and steep going up and she ran all the way here in her excitement."

He looked very mocking, she thought, sitting there in the wind, his shirt collar open, his hair blown hither and thither, the strong light of the newly released sun showing up the sardonic lines of his face. She lifted the child up to him and for a moment she looked him in the face; his eyes were bright, like those of a bird. She turned quickly and began hurrying up the steep path, the stones rolling dangerously from beneath her feet. She was repeating to herself what she had been muttering all morning.

"Don't forget to pack Hamish's other cloak and the bottle of cinnamon." All the way up the hill to the Manse she repeated the reminder, along beneath the gloom of the trees in the avenue she muttered it, in through the flat slab door and the dark hall, in through the swing door of the study. Then she remembered. She had packed everything long ago; there was no need to remember about the second cloak and the cinnamon; Hamish was gone. She sank down exhausted in his green leather chair, for she had come up the hill at a great pace.

She shook herself with impatience. What was the matter with her? Hamish had been away before; it was nothing, the time passed like lightning. Angrily she smoothed her hair. She heard the sound of the pony's feet on the drive. She went out to meet it; she invited Simon to share her meal. They talked gaily until the dark hardness of his face was gone and she saw only the light which danced in his eyes when he was amused.

Soon he departed, bowing in his charming stiff manner from the pony's back. She turned into the house once more, but all her fear had left her.

Chapter XII

IT took Hamish nine days to reach London from Leith, as the weather was fair. As they sailed up the Thames on the evening of the ninth day, he felt a stir within him. The light was beginning to fade and a blurred and rosy haze had descended on the river, the buildings floated like pleasure domes of Xanadu, everything seemed suspended. In the distance the hard shape of the new London Bridge was softened into deep shadowiness. As they sailed on, the river became more and more crowded with various craft, tacking here and there, now shooting forward through some gap, now standing irresolute with sails flapping this way and that in the breeze. Hamish was amazed at the skill of the men who handled these boats. The vision of the sound which lay between Glenlee and the Islands came to him suddenly, a great stretch of calmness, the mirror of mountains, the water lovingly translucent where the great shadows fell; he thought of the gray distance there, and the gleaming path of light cast

by the setting sun. He turned his eyes once
more to his surroundings. The width of the
brown water was strewn with feverishly hurrying craft, the small steamboats churning the
water furiously with their paddles; the sound
of hammering and of men's voices came out
across the water amid the creaking of sails and
spars. The indescribable river-smell, compo-
nent of tar and soot, and boats and drains, came
to him for the first time.

By the time they reached the Tower, the
light had almost gone, and red and green eyes
had begun to wink from the shadows. Shapes
slipped past them in the darkness. The Tower
loomed out on the north bank, white in the
half-light, fantastic. He had not expected it
to be so white, so like a child's toy; it was unlike
the grimness of the Highland castles when the
salt had eaten into the stone, until rock and
stone were almost one, and the whole was but
an abortive birth of the rocky mountainside.

They put in at a wharf near the Tower.
Strange faces were everywhere, strange oaths
filled the air; the English voices of his fellow
passengers, for they had picked up several on
their way down the east coast, seemed to divide
them from him; the strange smells which he

had never smelt before, added to his confusion.

Grasping his valise and other property, Hamish stepped ashore. Men rushed forward, quick and eager of speech, unlike his own Highlanders. They asked to carry his luggage and to guide him to his destination, but Hamish had heard of cut-throats and thieves; he grasped his valise the tighter and shook his head, pressing his arm to his sides to guard his inside pockets. The crowd jostled him and pushed him to and fro, until once he was quite near to the edge of the wharf; he could see the water black as oil down below, with golden streaks of fire dancing in it as it curled and gurgled round the landing-stage.

An overwhelming loneliness swept down on him. Who would know should he fall struggling into those dark waters? Who would know if he were led away and murdered in those narrow evil streets? He would lie naked and unwept for, and his face would never be seen again! He was quite clammy with the horror of his meditations. Most of the people had cleared off the wharf now, and Hamish saw a small fat man, hurrying up and down like an anxious hen; he was obviously seeking some one. Hamish had arranged to meet a Mr.

Towser, who was to give him lodging while he was in London. This Mr. Towser was a connection of the minister with whom Hamish had lodged in Edinburgh; he was a staunch Presbyterian, kept a flourishing grocer's shop and lived comfortably in Golden Square.

Hamish waited. Presently one of Mr. Towser's circles of search bulged in his direction. Mr. Towser stopped before him, raised his hat about an inch from his head and exactly parallel with it, his feet meanwhile continuing to move anxiously up and down.

"Sir," he said, addressing Hamish, "I am commissioned to find a gentleman of the name of McGregor." He pronounced the name with an emphasis upon the "Mac." "Something leads me to suppose that you are he."

Hamish bowed. The little man's filmy blue eyes were darting over his person almost as he himself had darted over the wharf. When Hamish had asserted his identity, the little man wrung him heartily by the hand for several seconds; each jerk of the arm seemed to jerk the words from his mouth, as though some carefully constructed automatic machine were functioning between hand and voice.

He was glad to see Hamish—he had almost

given up hope—the boat was late, the boat nearly always was; they would be home in time for refreshments at nine o'clock. He hoped Hamish had enjoyed his dinner; he had had a friend once who was practically starved on a voyage from Amsterdam to London. Yes, the luggage would be called for; he had thought Hamish would enjoy a stroll through the streets. In fact he was sure of this, so he had not ordered a conveyance.

Weary and bewildered, Hamish felt as though he must clap his hands over his ears. Always slow and thoughtful of speech, except when roused to anger or passionate emotion, he was swamped by the quick patter of Mr. Towser. He was averse to leaving his valise in such dark and gloomy surroundings. He followed his fat little guide silently, placed his valise in the comparative safety of a building which was labeled "office" but which bore no resemblance to an official building except this label.

They left the wharf and plunged into a network of narrow lanes which twisted in and out of one another in a bewildering maze. There seemed to be boats everywhere, and down at the foot of some of the sloping muddy alleys the masts and bowsprits seemed to have become

entangled with the crazy chimneys and windows
of the houses that flanked the river. The dank
smell of the river mingled with the unpleasant
stench of decaying filth. Through one of these
alleys Hamish caught sight of the new London
Bridge; he drew in his breath at the sight of the
arches; their strong curves thrilled him. His
companion pointed out the bridge to him
eagerly; he assured him that when the King
had opened it a year previously, the Thames
had been thronged so that there was only a
waterway of twenty feet through which the
royal barge had passed.

Once again they plunged into the dark narrow streets; above them was a strip of sky, clear
like opal. Suddenly they came out into King
William Street and crossed into the warren of
streets on the other side. There was silence in
the main thoroughfare, as it was too late for the
men to be working, but all was in process of
reconstruction; down by the bridge the new
Fishmongers' Hall was rising higher every day.
It all seemed terrific and poignant to Hamish;
he was treading the sacred stones which Chau-
cer, Milton, Shakespeare and Dr. Johnson had
trodden before him—he, Hamish McGregor, the

Minister of Glenlee, the tiny parish hidden away among the mountains and the mist.

They passed up the cobbles of Budge Row and down the narrow street which led into the still narrower Watling Street. Suddenly St. Paul's burst upon their sight. Hamish had caught a glimpse of it now and again, like a great dark purple bubble against the sky, and he had seen it from the river as the boat had drifted through the Port of London, but now it towered above him. He had never imagined its immensity. It was greater than he had thought possible. They hurried through St. Paul's Churchyard and down Ludgate Street, for it was growing dark rapidly and Mr. Towser began to glance about him sharply. He would have liked to call a hackney carriage, but he grudged expending the hard round coins which he could feel through the soft leather of his purse.

The brown of the brick houses on Ludgate Hill seemed evil to Hamish after the vision of St. Paul's; they were so close together, the whole thoroughfare must have measured less than sixteen yards across. Mr. Towser pointed out the Old Bailey to him, indicating the position of Newgate. Hamish, who had been very silent as he labored over the unaccustomed cobbles, suddenly burst forth at this, his great beautiful voice sounding oddly out of place among the ceaseless sounds of the city. He asked if there was any truth in the tale that the streets were thronged at an execution time. He received a reply in the affirmative, Towser adding innocently that he himself had attended the execution of Thurtell the murderer in the Twenties, and had paid a high price for a seat at a window in one of the neighboring houses.

Hamish paused, sickened for a moment. Here in the very shadow of St. Paul's, which he thought of as a crystallization of man's craving for beauty, the streets were thronged by evil eager humanity to watch a fellow human deprived of life. Everything seemed worthless and useless to him; the light faded from the bright gray eyes; he could not look at Mr. Towser's bird-like countenance; he hurried on in silence. At the bottom of the hill he turned to look back once more at St. Paul's. His view was slightly obstructed by the spire of St. Martin's Church, but it served only to intensify the magnificence and height of the dome. The light was almost gone now. The heavens were quiet, not a single cloud disturbed the vast expanse. One or two stars were appearing, and as he gazed more seemed to spring up from nowhere. An orange glow shone up from the murmuring city, cast by the lights which streamed from the windows into the streets; the form of the dome was softened by the dim light; even the cross on the top was blurred.

At the bottom of Fleet Street they passed under the stone arch of Temple Bar towards the Strand. Here Mr. Towser felt obliged to hail a passing vehicle to drive him to his home in Golden Square, the shadows really were so misleading, and it certainly was dark. Once upon a time the neighborhood round St. Clement's had been notorious for its evilness; he would not risk it, even though it was almost physical pain to him to part with his hard round coins.

That night, as he lay in bed at the top of the house in Golden Square, Hamish was filled with elation and yet with a hurried fluttering fear. He wanted something which he could not name. Perhaps it was the sound of the sea; perhaps it was the wet salt smell of seaweed which haunts the west coast of Scotland—he could not tell, but his heart seemed to bleed, although it throbbed with joy. To-morrow he would visit great houses and rich men, who would give him money for his starving parishioners; he would obtain the lymph soon; he would see Westminster and Apsley House, perhaps even the Iron Duke himself; then he would sail home; he would land a hero, a man great and wise who has traveled; he could almost hear the people's voices acclaiming him.

Then the vision of the Glenlee sound and the hills of the Islands clouded out everything else and his Highland eyes filled with tears. He prayed long and earnestly and then fell asleep.

Hamish was in London for six weeks, during which time he visited the "vanities" of the city; the glistening shop windows bulging forward into the streets delighted him against his will. One day he stood beside the gates of St. James's Palace to watch the splendor and nobility of England stream forth to attend a grand levee. He stood for almost two hours, the splendor of the horses and the beauty of the women filling his mind with wonder and enthusiasm; it seemed to him that the streets of London were indeed paved with gold, that poverty was unknown. He watched in a dream, the everlasting stream of gold and silver, velvet and ostrich feathers; he was a boy again perusing "The Arabian Nights" for the first time. But this was all unreal, fantastic, it seemed to him that he had but to touch the gleaming carriages and they would dissolve into nothing, and the brightly dressed inmates would fall to the ground like dusty unused marionettes, their limbs stiff and wooden under the velvet and lace. He could not take all this grandeur as something real; only tar-smelling boats were real and Church Session Registers and his dolphin tobacco jar and things of that kind. Allison, his wife, was real, so real that she hardly seemed to exist at all.

One day he stood on Westminster Bridge looking out on the City. He stood in one of the little alcoves which the old bridge boasted. Just so had Wordsworth stood some thirty years before and gazed over the silent City, offering its domes, palaces and theaters to the smokeless air. Westminster Hall was on his right hand; his feelings with regard to this edifice, where the government of the country sat in majesty, were indescribable. On the previous day he had stood in the lobby of the House of Commons experiencing the satisfying thrill of a lifelong desire fulfilled. He wrote afterwards to Allison: *"As we stood in the lobby, occasional glances of the interior were obtained when the large folding-doors, which shut of themselves, were pushed open by some members entering the great forum of the world, the limb of the Universe; as I stood there my heart thrilled."*

As he stood on the bridge afterwards, his eyes wandered proudly towards the somewhat insignificant building—the double-towered frontage of Westminster Abbey could be clearly seen over the sloping roof. Traffic rumbled ceaselessly over the narrow bridge; everything seemed surging with life; he alone stood idle, watching the water flow silently beneath the many arches and the sun go flaring to rest in the west.

Chapter XIII

In the meantime summer was beginning to pass into autumn up in the glen. It was still summer, but when the dusk began to fall the dew was heavier and frost seemed to be lurking somewhere. The colors grew richer every day; the bracken was golden on the hillside and the rowan berries such a vital scarlet that it almost took the breath away to look at them. Every evening the sun sank over the western islands in such beauty that it left Allison's mind curiously blank, yet filled with an inexpressible sense of splendor. The flaring islands of cloud, silhouetted against the translucent sea of gold and crimson which deepened and grew richer as the path of light disappeared from the water, would seem eternal, perfect in form, and quite motionless, and then quite quickly they would crumble together in great blazing ruins, and presently the sky would be vast and lonely, a wild duck-egg blue.

The rain-sodden mist-encircled glen of the winter months might have been a figment of her own brain; the sun rose each day in a cloudless blue heaven, and the distant hills shimmered in the haze. These were happy days. She missed Hamish, but the children seemed so joyous. When Jean recited the verses of the Psalms that she had learned, her large gray eyes seemed alive with joy; she almost sang the words, her eyes wandering from one object to another, her mind far away.

Alex, too, would sing and chuckle to himself, repeating a word over and over again in sheer joy of the sound, while he sat on the grass among the whin bushes behind the house, the sun gleaming on his hair so that it appeared beautiful. Even David, the baby, seemed to feel something of the peace and sunshine. He would lie in his crib, closing and unclosing his chubby little hands as he stretched them towards the shafts of sunlight; his solemn brown face, with its dark eyes, would suddenly break into a smile. When Allison picked him up and carried him outside, he would stretch out his hands for everything, making queer little sounds to express his content.

Allison knew in her heart of hearts that it was fear that had been removed from the house. The children feared Hamish, with his sudden

bursts of rage and quick commands. He seldom
smiled at them, regarding them seriously as the
gifts of God. He was never cruel, but there was
a hard core to his nature which his wife had
discovered more than once; it was born of his
reverence for the God of the Old Testament.
Life was real and earnest, and children, as part
of life, must be prepared for it. Solemnly he
told Jean of the grave and of eternal punish-
ment, of the Day of Judgment, so that the baby
mind always felt an overhanging fear; now that
he was gone, some of that fear seemed to be
gone as well. Life must be great, beautiful and
clean, not the miserable sordid thing that men
made it. Hamish believed this with every fiber
of his being, and he strove with all his might to
make things more beautiful according to his
own criterion; in so doing he robbed his own
children of the beauty of life which children
alone know, and which is too intense to last,
the beauty of a vision. They were taught to
fear evil and its consequences, not to despise it;
thus they searched for it fearfully where it did
not exist.

Andrew Simon's foot was mending slowly.
He spent long days fishing in the bay or in the
neighboring lochs; he would come up to the

Manse in the evening when Allison sat alone
sewing. He talked rapidly, hardly waiting for
her to reply. He, too, seemed happy. His
courtesy was perfect; he was charming, fascinat-
ing; her heart would leap as she heard the sound
of his limping footsteps and the tap of his stick.
He never flattered her now, but somehow he
was much nearer to her than before, even
though she only saw him in the evenings. Sometimes he did not come, and when she asked him
on the next evening where he had been, he
never seemed to know: time was nothing to him.
He loved the children and would play for hours
with them; sometimes Allison would watch
them unobserved. One day she saw him pick
up Jean as she stood before him, rowan berries
crushed in her small hot hand; he tossed her in
the air gleefully and then kissed her in an ecstasy
of delight, rubbing his cheek against her soft
hair; Allison saw the look of contentment and
joy on his face and sighed.

On other occasions he sat as though the children did not exist for him. They would speak
to him, and he would hardly answer; sometimes
he would even push them aside; suddenly he
would rise and limp away, leaving the children to
their own devices, often leaving them in danger

by forgetting to shut the gate which prevented the Highland cattle from infringing upon the whin coppice. On these days his eyes were hard and the lines about his mouth more marked.

One day about the middle of September Allison heard his footsteps on the drive earlier than usual. It was still cool, and the sun not having reached its height, she was sitting in the parlor mending the napery; it was dark in there and the shafts of sunlight made it difficult to see such fine work. He halted in the hall and called her, then he came into the parlor. He had discarded his stick now, and although his limp was greater than it had been before his accident, he was almost recovered. He was in one of his brightest and most charming moods; he had come to ask her and the children to accompany him on a picnic.

During the weeks of Hamish's absence the silence and power of the wild landscape seemed to have crept into his mind, so that its gray tide swept away the trivialities of everyday life. They disappeared on the onrushing tide like ugly dancing motes. During the long days that he spent fishing or tramping the hills (this was still tedious work to him, for his ankle ached after any exertion) his active mind was lulled

into an acceptance of life as it was. The beat
of the soft Highland rain upon his face, as it
scudded across the wrinkled sea, made him rejoice. Down in the dark waters of Loch Scavaig,
with the sound of the waves dashing on the
rocky shore, he would watch with fascination
the interchange of light and cloud on the
Coolins far above him; the peak of Scurr
Alistair and the ugly jagged gap of Bruach-na-
frith would appear and disappear in the mist.
The legion of great gray rain-clouds would blot
out the splintered heights for a moment and
then the curtain would split, revealing a tiny
gap of duck-egg blue. Then above the gray,
the light would shine out, edging the billowing
mass with a white radiance, until the whole
mistiness dissolved, and the sun shone out clear
on the white clouds and the clear blue of the
heavens, lighting up little patches of the hillside with a yellowish glow. The waters of the
loch would be transformed into a glittering
blue; even when he climbed the rocky ridge that
divided Scavaig from Coruisk, and looked down
on its gloomy waters, the sun seemed to have
lent a kind of transparence to the depths. Then
suddenly the mist would close in again and he
would be surrounded by a swirling mass, and by

black gleaming precipices; in a second he would be drenched by the driving rain.

On these occasions, when he ventured to distant lochs, he sailed a tiny fishing smack; sometimes he took Donald McAllister with him, but more often he went by himself. Sometimes coming round the point of Sleat the Atlantic force seemed to hurl itself at the puny boat, and more than once he had stayed out all night, unable to brave the roaring tides and winds; but more often there was no more than a gentle ground swell, and the atmosphere was so clear that the Islands of Rum and Canna seemed only a mile or two away. It seemed to Andrew Simon as he sat idly fishing, his fingers fumbling with the wet lengths of deep-sea line, that a sort of meaning was creeping into life, a vague pattern, which was on such a gigantic scale that its symmetry was lost. A human soul, working its tiny way along its tiny thread of life, was like an insect crawling over a vast patterned carpet; when the tiny thing was on a dark square, all around it seemed dark, its progress across the blackness seemed everlasting, it could not see the balanced colors all round the black square, the diamonds of crimson or chains of green and yellow; perhaps it might never reach them, but that made no difference to the existence of the patterned carpet.

It was easier in the quiet of this Hebridean scenery to imagine the scheme of life as a balanced pattern, to see events that had tortured him and overwhelmed him as black squares, taking their place among brighter squares. The misery of the war which had ceased so long ago, but had left a disgusted horror in his mind, grew less, and the starvation and slavery of the working classes ceased to oppress him in the way it had done. Social trouble was the necessary outcome of the war, and war was the necessary outcome of human nature. He was convinced that the elemental passions of human nature, although good, were bound to the weak animal instincts of fear and greed as well as to the good ones. Fear and greed were the fundamental causes of war, and as long as humans were human there would be no averting strife. Human nature did not progress, in his estimation; there were great streaks of nobility in every age, different types of nobility. If human nature did progress, then the change, like that of mountains and oceans, was imperceptible.

Perhaps this severity to which the race was

subjected, the severity of starvation and oppression, fitted into the pattern. Perhaps it would produce a stronger race both mentally and physically. Those that were unfit in body would never survive the struggle. Would not strength of body produce strength of mind? Even now were they not entering a new era? The Reform Bill had been passed in June: was it not the herald of a brighter square in the pattern? Those who had died in the darkness of the previous square would not know of it, but it would exist. And then he would remember individuals and details which swept away the roots of his new-found philosophy. The dying child he had seen in a Renfrewshire village, its frame wasted to nothing, its body crooked with the strain of labor, and then the contrast of his father's table, loaded with food and gleaming silver, and his father with servants running to and fro at his command, the splendor of banquets and the gold on gaming tables. He knew that there must be rich and poor, but must the gap between them be so terrific? He would remember the war again. That young Peterson screaming at the other side of the orchard at Hougoumont, his round childish face twisted in agony, his high, almost feminine voice cracked with anguish, his hands clutching at his shattered shoulder, his maimed arm mauled and bloody at his side.

But beyond all these cruel incidents which came back to his mind unbidden, a steady gleam appeared; it was often shrouded as the peaks of the Coolins were, but it would appear again and again, and he was conscious of its image even when it was obscured. He was conscious of a moving spirit behind the earth; everything that surrounded him seemed to bear truth to it: the minute petals and stamens of the tiny creeping tormentil, or the magic colors and fins of the mackerel and codling, the form of the clouds and the hills, and again the spirit which triumphed in man, struggling against the obliterating and wearing monotony of life. This was the spirit which drove men to discover in unknown lands, to write great poems, paint great pictures, and to keep their heads ever above the water in their own individual ocean. He admitted to himself that all the beauty of the earth could be reasonably and scientifically explained, the formation of the mountains, the colors of the fish, the shape of the flowers; but could every human action be traced to fundamental animal instincts? He did not recognize anything so concrete as a God; a man-made criterion of right and wrong did not enter into such a vast conception; he did not seek to crystallize his conviction of a driving force; he believed it to be a force far above human realization. The attempt to understand such a force was like a gnat attemping to work out a mathematical problem; the problem was infinitely beyond the capacity of the brain. He felt that man could go no further than to realize his own minuteness, and to realize that to form a force into a God, an idealized edition of himself, was a blasphemy.

The new-found conviction of the hidden fire in human nature opened his mind towards Allison. She was the only intelligent human being to whom he talked in these days, when the loneliness and static quality of the Highland fastnesses was inspiring him with new confidence. Her youth seemed sacred to him, and the courage and calmness which shone in her brown eyes seemed a crystallization of the attitude to which he strove to attain. Her simplicity seemed to him beautiful, after the duplicity and tawdry value of many of the women he had met; her gentle restfulness was lovely to him. She fitted into his dream of a wider philosophy.

When she was afraid, and sometimes he had
seen fear creep into her eyes, he longed to comfort her as one comforts a child. Sometimes he
longed to make love to her, she was so very
beautiful, and almost tantalizing in her lack of
coquetry; it seemed to him that she thought of
everything as having a hard and fast outline,
right and wrong, life and death. She was married to Hamish, therefore no other man could
have part in her life. She treated him as he
had never been treated by a woman before,
with unaffected frankness. If he leaned over
the back of the chair in which she sat, to look
at what she was reading, she would turn her
face to his with the simplicity of a child and bid
him sit beside her where he could see better.
It seemed to him that the only barrier between
them was the code of manners to which she had
been brought up; she would offer him her hand
frankly when she climbed over a dyke, only remembering in sudden fits and starts that he was
a strange man and she a married woman.

He had caught her sitting on the floor more
than once; sometimes she would not realize her
position for a minute or two, so natural was she
in his presence. Then suddenly, the crimson
flooding her neck, she would realize and spring

to her feet, overcome with confusion, remembering that she was the Minister's wife and he a guest, of a sex apart.

Lately, however, she had seemed abstracted, and once or twice she had been out when he visited the Manse; he began to wonder if she had realized the state of his feelings. It almost made him smile to think of her horror-struck expression if she should discover that he was in love with her; not for one moment did it enter his head that Allison herself, bewildered and filled with an unaccustomed joy, was falling in love with him with all the strength of her quiet innocent nature. She did not realize it herself, because it seemed incredible, a wickedness beyond comprehension.

At first Allison would not accept the invitation to the picnic; Hamish, she felt, would not like it; she had never been out alone with Simon, except for a short stroll up Ben Buie or down to the sea; a picnic was rather an unusual proceeding, all sorts of objections passed through her mind; but he begged her with such impetuosity that in the end she gave in to him and went in search of provisions to take with them.

The children were wild with excitement; all

the way down to the shore Jean danced ahead
of them, while Alex ran uncertainly behind her,
his sturdy legs flinging sideways and backwards
in a frenzy of haste.

The boat which Simon had hired was a heavy
lug-sail; the sail was old and had been carefully
patched, but the boat was newly tarred and var-
nished and gave out a pleasant smell as it lay
in the sun. Once afloat, all misgiving left Allison; she loved the sea when it lay like a shining
plain of glass, the white reflections of the clouds
moving slowly in its depths. The sound of the
water slipping gently away from the prow, as
the sail filled with the faint breeze, delighted
her. The children trailed their fingers in the
water, so that their sleeves were soon soaked;
all the time they talked and exclaimed, calling
to the seagulls which hovered above the little
craft and then swooped away with wild lost cries.

They glided down the sound, the far islands
misty on the blue horizon; they turned into
Loch Doul and landed in a little bay, which
shone with white sand. The mountains towered
above them, free of mist. They ate their meal
on the shore.

When they had finished, the children scam-
pered away to the sea's edge once more; their

little figures could be seen stooping over heavy seaweed-covered boulders which they rolled aside to find the brown squirming butter-eels.

Simon lay in his favorite attitude, flat on his back, his knees crooked up; the sun poured down on his face. Allison sat beside him, her full skirt spread out round her, her small feet just peeping from beneath; she would have liked to take off her bonnet, but she did not think that she ought. A wild desire to paddle passed through her mind at one moment, but of course that was quite out of the question: there was no chance of ridding herself of Simon for a safe enough length of time; and, besides, what would Hamish say, did he know that she had paddled within three or four miles of the Manse door? A slight smile crept over her face.

"What are you smiling at?" said Simon, opening his eyes at that moment.

Allison blushed. Suddenly he made up his mind. Why should he not make love to her? She was too lovely to be resisted. He sat up beside her and said in delighted tones: "It entertains me beyond measure when you blush like that."

Allison was overcome, her face was crimson, she could feel the blood suffusing her neck, she felt as though she must be blushing all over; she turned away from him in distress.

"I must beg your pardon," he said, smiling. "I didn't mean to confuse you, but you look so monstrously like Jean when you blush."

Allison did not smile, but looked away from him. He was silent for a moment or two; when he spoke again his tone was different, he regarded her rather wistfully.

"Before I go from Glenlee," he said, "I want to thank you for all you have done for me."

Allison turned towards him surprised. "But you're not going yet?" she said quickly, and then rather breathlessly: "I am afraid we haven't entertained you sufficiently; it was so unfortunate your breaking that ankle and Hamish's having to go to Edinburgh. It was a pleasure for us to have you as our visitor. Hamish has so few people to talk to up here; I often fear he must be lonely."

Simon turned over on his side and regarded her seriously. "And you?" he said. "Is it not lonely for you?"

She did not answer for a moment; then she said rather suddenly: "Yes, I am lonely sometimes, but in a different way. You see, I'm not clever and so the conversation of the country people is very satisfying to me—and of course I always have the children round me."

"Then why are you lonely?" said Simon bluntly, still looking at her.

She gave him a troubled glance, like a perplexed child that does not know how to describe what is wrong with it.

"Sometimes," she said, plucking a sprig of ragwort and pulling out the yellow tufts from the flower, "I feel sad, and wonder about things that are too—too silly to bother Hamish with. And when I have nobody to discuss them with, I feel lonely, as though I were the only person in the world with these odd thoughts." She smiled at him then, excusing her silliness, but he did not smile back.

"Before I was married I had sisters to whom I could talk of these silly fancies, and so I forgot about them and seemed to share them with other people. Sometimes it seems like a dream, the life before I came here. The parish from which we came was well populated with gentry as well as fisher-folk, and I had neighbors who would often come and take tea with me, and we would gossip and sew and discuss the children; and some of them were so pretty," she added inconsequently.

"And now," said Simon, "you never see another woman to whom you can talk as an equal, or to whom you can show your pretty new lilac frock, and so—you have to talk to me." He threw back his head and gave one of his sudden husky laughs.

"Why, I'm sure you're very kind to listen to me," she said hastily. "I hadn't meant to say so much, but you are always so polite and pretend to be interested that I forget how I am chattering." She turned her head away from him again and her mouth trembled.

Suddenly she felt him take her hand; with round frightened eyes she saw him stoop forward and kiss it.

"I take it as a very great honor," he said, "that you allow me to do this."

She thought to herself that she had not had much choice in the matter, but she did not say so.

"You have brought something into my life which had departed years ago, a belief in good women."

"You call me a good woman!" exclaimed Allison, drawing away her hand, which she had allowed to remain in his. "Why, if you only knew how rebellious I am, how selfish! I appear meek, but the things I think are sometimes really wicked."

He smiled at her, delighted with her naivety.

"Allison," he said softly—it was the first time he had used her Christian name, but neither of them noticed it—"I've seen so much wickedness and suffering when I've been campaigning abroad, or when I've left the brightly lighted thoroughfares in London, that I think your wickedness would not appal me."

She took no notice of him, but clasping her small hands together she said firmly: "There is a special wickedness that threatens each individual person, and comparing it with other people's does not lessen it. If things exist nothing can lessen them."

"And what wickedness threatens you, monstrous and black-dyed villainess?" inquired Simon, amused at her fervor.

"Please don't laugh at me," she pleaded, giving him an upward glance of her soft eyes which sent a strange shiver down his spine. "It isn't just silly little things that I'm wicked over. I don't know what evil thing I shall do next; I have to cling onto real things sometimes, because I'm afraid I'll do something which would cause sorrow to both myself and other people."

Simon was serious now. He rose to his feet and limped a few paces off. He stood regarding the shimmering water of the loch; then he turned and came back to her.

"When Hamish went away," he said, "did you ask that I might be sent down to McAllister's?"

Allison flushed and cast down her eyes. How had he guessed this? She was utterly at a loss. She muttered something about Hamish's not thinking it suitable that he should stay; but he would not be put off, he stood above her frowning.

"Allison, answer me," he said.

Timidly she stole a glance at him, then she said in a voice that trembled, "Yes, I suggested it to him."

"Were you so afraid of me, then?" asked Simon.

But she would not answer him; tears gleamed on her lashes. When she looked at him again his face seemed lit up with joy; she could not understand his excitement.

He was suddenly aware that she loved him.

At half-past five they stood up to go. A heavy bank of mist rolled into the loch, a faint breeze blew from the land. The silence was unearthly. Allison stood gazing across at the mountain-tops, merging from the bank of hurrying clouds; first they were obscured and then the mist was torn asunder and they towered out hard and immovable once more.

Suddenly she felt his hands on her shoulders, she knew that his face was very close to hers; she stood silent, immovable, her mind empty of every sensation except that he was so standing. The blood seemed to be racing through her body; very gently his arms closed round her, then his fingers fumbled at her bonnet strings and she felt the breeze on her bare head, his cheek was against hers and then she felt him kissing her hair; instinctively he knew how to make love to her so that she melted to his touch. She stood so still that he was alarmed.

"Allison, beloved, what is it?" he whispered; his husky eager voice trembled with the tensity of his feelings.

The sound of his voice seemed to jerk something in her brain. With a smothered little cry she turned to him and he took her in his arms. Her face was dead white and her eyes were closed. She did not resist in his arms. He stroked her hair, murmuring endearments; she was silent.

"My dear, I love you," he said softly.

She opened her eyes then and answered—the words were so low he could scarcely hear them. "Yes, that's it," she murmured. "That's what it was. I loved you." Her voice sounded dazed and hard.

He led her down to the water's edge. The lug-sail was high and dry, lying drunkenly on her side. Simon had meant to drag her down, little by little as the tide went out, but his mind had worked in one excited circle all the afternoon, the image of Allison's hands, the curve of her cheek, her slow childish smile, obsessed his powers of vision. No wonder, then, that the boat lay high and dry among the seaweed. He strained fruitlessly at it, moving it inch by inch; the sweat stood on his brow so that his damp hair clung to it in sticky twists. At first Allison watched him, then she laid her firm little hands on the gunwale and dragged with him. He smiled at her over the width of the boat, and his dark eyes were deep and melting. A sudden surge of joy overwhelmed Allison. Until that moment she had seemed turned to stone; now life flowed back into her veins, and an urgency of feeling which almost hurt in its intensity; her eyes stung with sharp emotional tears. She was conscious of a terrible aching fear which lay just below the surface of her brain, a dark sea of horror tossing and reaching towards her to engulf her forever, but this was divided from her by a thin golden haze which transformed all into beauty. The tide had turned now, and was creeping up to meet them. They moved the heavy boat slowly and sat down to rest often. Allison's hands, unaccustomed to manual labor of a severe kind, were beginning to smart and blister; she stretched out her fingers, puckering up her mouth. In delight Simon stooped down and kissed her fingers; she felt his head against her breast; she did not protest.

The world seemed unreal to her; the mist lay on the water a few yards away, blotting out the opposite shore of the loch. The silence was intense, they might have been the only inhabitants of a vast and lonely planet. The continuous ripple of the water breaking on the stones seemed to lull her into semi-consciousness. She smiled down on him like a sleepy child, stroking his hair with her free hand. And all the time that dark sea churned to and fro in her mind, and terror hurried towards her.

At last the boat was launched; Simon stood in the water up to his knees, steadying her on

upright keel, whilst Allison lifted in the sleepy
children. Alex laid his head on her shoulder
as she lifted him up, and would have fallen
asleep had she not put him down inside the
boat. It was a difficult matter dragging the boat
off the ground, but at last it was effected, and
she drifted out into the mist, the water lap-
lapping against her sides. There was no breath
of wind, the world had died. Simon took the
oars and began to row; the water ran along the
blades as he held them suspended in the air
and dripped silently into the glass-smooth water.
The light was dim.

Allison sat in the stern. Alex slept against
her shoulder, his fair sun-bleached head appearing wanly in the faint magical light.

Allison spoke in a whisper, and Simon's an-
swers were in the same low key; then they re-
lapsed into silence. After what seemed an
eternity the water about them began to hurry
and swirl as though agitated by unseen agencies,
and they knew that they must be in the bay of
Glenlee.

Simon pulled across the current, working
hard with his port oar. In the silence they
could hear the water roaring and sighing as the

tide rushed through the narrows ahead of them. The sound was threatening and strange.

"They say that drowning is a pleasant death," murmured Simon, "an easy death—have you ever wanted to die?"

Allison raised her eyes, startled. "No," she said very low. "I am afraid of death."

"Nobody knows what it is," continued Simon slowly. "Eternal nothingness? Or is there some enormous physical convulsion? Once I wanted to die, but I was afraid to, because I didn't know."

There was a silence and then Allison said slowly, "And after death there is Heaven and Hell." She said this in a hard little voice. "And eternal damnation."

He stared at her, bewildered. "My dear," he said, "you do not believe that?"

She looked at him in mute agony and the hungry tossing sea in her mind drew nearer the surface. She stretched out her hand to him and said very low, "Not when I am with you."

Presently the keel grated on the shore, and through the mist the dark shapes of the crofts were visible. Simon moored the boat, and taking Alex in his arms limped beside Allison up the hill to the Manse. The damp air enveloped them, and the tendrils of Allison's hair clung to her cheeks.

They came to the expressionless slab of the Manse front door; the silence was still all round them save for the lost bleating of the lambs on the side of Ben Buie and the sound of the water falling into the linn behind the house.

Before Allison knocked, for the door was barred, as it was past nine o'clock, she glanced across at Simon. His eyes were devouring her and the hard bird-like look was in them; he stretched out his hand to caress her cheek, the hard excited look in his eyes growing. He drew her to him and she felt his hand sliding caressingly from her waist over her thighs, then suddenly his head dropped and she saw the tears in his unhappy eyes. Her mouth sought his hair, she loved him as she had never loved before. They stood there in the dusk.

Jean stood on tiptoe, but she could not reach the knocker. Exasperated, she beat with her small fists on the door. Bella's heavy footsteps echoed through the hall and the door was thrown open. It was dark inside the hall.

"The mist kept us back, Bella," said Allison quietly.

Simon handed the sleeping Alex to Bella; his head fell forward on her ample bosom.

Allison turned quickly.

"Good night," she said, and was gone.

After he had gone, Allison pushed open the swing door into Hamish's study. The lamp was burning there; it cast its light on the green chair and the bookcases and the dolphin tobacco jar.

She stood irresolute in the middle of the room; then suddenly the dark sea which had been tossing and swirling in her mind engulfed her; she was drowning, she was lost, she trembled from head to foot. Till now she had refused to face things; now, all alone in the chilly study, she set out to do it.

At eleven o'clock she rose and went up to bed; her face looked haggard in the candlelight. She had reached two pinnacles of emotion in twelve hours which she was never to touch again in the whole course of her existence, that of pure happiness and that of a wild despair caused by her own choosing.

Down on the wall which divided the road from the shore, Andrew Simon sat and smoked his pipe. The beauty of the evening soaked into his mind. The mist had risen and stars were coming out in the fairy blue of the sky; the white line of foam where the waves broke was ghostly in the half-light, the sea itself was dark and mysterious. His spirit went out to the world about him. Joy possessed him.

Chapter XIV

THE next morning broke stormy, and rain fell on the parched land for the first time for many days. Water raced down the sides of the hill road, the burn roared down the steeps of Ben Buie, hurling itself in a brown creaming mass into the linn. Leaves were torn from the trees, the sea was dark, casting up dollops of evil yellow foam. The mountains of the Islands were blurred by the clouds of rain and mist. The air was full of the sound of hurrying waters once again.

Simon sat beside the peat fire in McAllister's croft. He had finished his porridge and the bowl stood beside him on the floor; he kicked the peats idly with his foot. Water was trickling down the walls, and the draught, which raced in beneath the door, stirred the bedraggled hangings of the box-bed in the corner. The sound of Morag, Donald's wife, washing the dishes came from the other room. Simon dreamed on undisturbed.

Suddenly the door burst open and a man

precipitated himself into the room; gusts of rain followed him, and the boom of the sea filled the cottage. With difficulty he reclosed the door. It was John, the man from the Manse. From the dark recesses of his person he produced a letter which he handed to Simon.

"I wis tae say that there would be no need of an answer," he said, as though repeating some weighty and difficult proverb. He wiped the rain from his eyes and then turned and went out again, touching his forelock.

Simon carried the letter to the tiny window; it was so dark in the croft that he could not see to read. It was neatly folded and addressed to him in Allison's fine Italian hand. The rain rattled on the window in a sudden onslaught. He opened the letter slowly and began to read. He read it through twice before its full meaning broke upon him. Absently he stuffed the letter into his pocket and stood gazing through the tiny panes at the rain-dimmed seascape. There was a flaw in one of the panes which swirled and distorted his line of vision.

The letter ran thus:

I cannot see you again; I cannot explain why this is so, but I feel that it will be better. Per-

haps it is because I am a coward. I think I shall never care for any one in the world as I have come to care for you, but there are my children and I am a married woman; if I go they are left; they are mine, flesh of my flesh, and I cannot leave them.

During the last month you have made me happier than I thought it was possible to be. I am the cause of adding misery to a life which has been too much filled with it already; I feel that I would die willingly to add happiness to your life and yet I wilfully inflict misery upon you.

We cannot see one another again. There is a boat coming into the bay at noon to take on the emigrants.

Someday it may be clearer to us both, when we are older and the children grown men and women; but whatever I do, I do it because I believe it to be best, and I think I shall love you until I die. May the Lord have mercy on sinners.

This letter does not express what is in my mind, but perhaps you will find some meaning in it.

May God bless and protect you.

Allison.

The staccato agonized phrases of the letter repeated themselves in Simon's brain. So she preferred her children to him! Well, it was all to be expected; life was rotten and ugly, it always had been. Every connection was to be severed. He was to go away and never be heard of again; she would go on living her old life. She had played with him, egged him on. But even as these thoughts rushed through his mind he knew that they were untrue; her life would never be the same, she had sought to escape from him, but forces had been too strong for her.

"If only I could see her," he muttered, drawing the back of his hand across his brow in distraction. How hard she was! How cruel, to send him away without so much as a farewell. Tears came into his eyes; he was worn out by the cruelty of life and its never-ending and fatal jesting. In his heart of hearts he knew that she was right; she had a strength in her which he lacked. If they were to part, then there was no good playing with their torn emotions; it was terrible, devastating. He flung himself down on the seat beside the fire and buried his face in his hands. Why were things so wrong, why were all standards reversed? Allison and he

were made for happiness, they had the intense appreciation of joy which was denied to so many, why should they not seek their happiness? But, then, their happiness was the unhappiness of others. There seemed no answer to anything; he felt himself being crushed out of existence by vast forces. He wanted Allison so much that he could not keep still; he moved up and down the kitchen and then he flung outside into the wind.

He had been wounded like this before, but this time it was not only his vanity that was hurt—there was something indefinable which cried out in his mind. The Manse stood up on the hillside; he could not bear to look at it.

At twelve o'clock the ship which was to call for the emigrants came into view. The shore was blackened by a dark mass of people. There were six young men going away. Simon stood alone, outside the throng. He felt numb and bitter. Why should he go away? Even now he longed to rush up to the Manse, take her in his arms and explain how the agony of leaving her was tearing him to pieces. Surely she would relent; she who would weep at the sight of a dead animal, how could she bear to see him tortured? He climbed slowly into the rowing boat with three of the young men.

The crowd on the shore were moaning now in a weird hopeless way; tears streamed down the cheeks of the men who were leaving the only land they knew; a bewildered horror was depicted on their bronzed faces, and in their gray eyes. The setting was perfect, the waves dashed against the boat's side and boomed on the shore, the gulls screamed and wailed. To Simon it all seemed a mockery, a terrible reality set in all the gewgaws of theatrical sorrow; the moan of the people and the tears of the men infuriated him.

The ship tore before the wind; with a wild straining of the sails it passed the headland.

In the Manse parlor, Allison sat sewing. The window did not look out towards the sea; the headland was only visible from the window of her bedroom; she did not go upstairs. Nevertheless she seemed to hear the noise of the waves and the flapping of the sails, and above all the husky eager voice imploring her; she bowed her head. Why had she sent him away like that? She had run away from her own happiness, she had hurt him, spoilt the beauty of the world for him—perhaps he would forget—and

for what had she exchanged her happiness? For nothing, for nothing, for another man's caresses. She shuddered at the thought. Before her stretched an eternity of darkness and fear without happiness. A wild terror overtook her. She caught up her shawl and hurried outside; she stumbled through the trees, panting as she went, uttering his name in heartbroken tones. She pushed her way through the brambles; the sea and the hills of the Islands burst upon her vision, and streaming steadily from the bay she could see the black crowd of mourning people. The sea was deserted; the ship had passed out of sight

Chapter XV

HAMISH was fishing for flounders up beyond the sound. He had brought McAllister to row for him. It was a fine autumn afternoon, but the sun was already crimson and so low that the sea was golden as it stretched hazily away towards the Atlantic, yet it was only three o'clock. The wooden box with a glass bottom, which served to still the tremor of the water, was heavy to press down on the surface. When Hamish looked through it he could still see the bed of the ocean, the faint movement of the brown seaweed, as it floated upwards from its root, the limpet-covered rocks and the sudden swirl of sand where a flounder lay hidden. But it was much darker now, and the colors under the sea had all merged into one brownish, neutral tint. His right hand was numb as it gripped the long two-pronged spear, his left hand was swollen with the salt water. The bottom of the boat was silvered with the scales of the fish he had caught. They lay in heaps, some on their backs so that the blue-

whiteness of their bellies shone in the shadow.
Reluctantly Hamish dragged the glass-bottomed
box over the side and took one of the oars from
Donald. It was good to feel the blood flowing
in his numbed hands and arms once more.

The boat moved swiftly towards the kyle; the
two men were facing the sunset. Saya and
Rhena loomed a soft dark purple, a steady light
shone from a cottage on the point. The rocky
scraps of Islands across the strait looked like odd
prehistoric sea-monsters. The darkness seemed
almost to move about them, so rapidly did it
fall.

The western sky was a vast lonely arch of
transparent yellow, as though a great light
burned far away behind it; the soft blurred
flames of the sun as it rested on the horizon
seemed to spill over into the sea, suffusing it
with light. Near at hand all was dark, and the
great forms of the mountains rose on every side.
The oars made a phosphorescent cloud of silver
under the water, and when the rowers paused,
the drops from their oars hung like diamonds
or tiny globes of fire.

As they passed through the kyle, where the
water was beginning to whisper and hurry with
the turn of the tide, the lights from Glenlee

came suddenly into view.   Up on the hillside
the Manse windows gleamed through the trees.

Something moved in Hamish's heart. He had
been back from London six weeks now, but
still he was stirred by the sight of Glenlee.
When he had sailed into the bay six weeks ago
on just such an evening as this, he had felt a
sudden love which seemed to come from his
very body. The crunch of the stones beneath
his feet as he landed had filled him with a
delirious joy, and the smell of the damp rotting
seaweed. As he had lain in bed that night,
through the window he heard the solitary lost
cry of a whaup which seemed to intensify the
magnificent silence. It seemed to him then that
his heart would burst with happiness. Allison
had been asleep beside him, but he had taken
her in his arms so fiercely that he had wakened
her. She had lain there quite passive, but a
kind of chill seemed to pass to him; he had
looked into her eyes startled, they were wide
and dark like the eyes of a rabbit in a snare.
He had drawn her to his breast so that he should
not see them. He hoped that another son
would be born because of the glorious passion
he had felt that night; his heart warmed towards
this unborn son as it had never done towards

Alex and the baby David. Sometimes he thought of those dull wide eyes which had looked at him from the white oval of Allison's face, and of the curious feeling of holding something lifeless in his arms, but he did not allow such things to trouble him long.

All day long he had been busy assisting in the vaccination of the people, persuading them, and explaining away their superstitious dread. He had vaccinated his own children, having learned the art carefully from a London surgeon. Jean had wept silently, and Alex had roared until his fat little face was purple with emotion, and great round tears rolled down the side of his nose. But the baby David, after one sudden little whimper, had lain quite still and silent, and it seemed to Hamish that there was mockery in his dark hazel eyes, which of course was impossible, the child was not a year old. This child of his always disturbed him; perhaps it was because he was so unlike him in appearance, so unlike the other two children, with their wide gray eyes and light flaming hair. He was solemn, yet uncannily observant for a child so young.

Hamish had set the crofters working on the causeway in the bay; even now, as he walked up towards the Manse, he could see the outline of unbroken piles of rock against the sea. The men had collected the material there in preparation for laying the foundation. Hamish sighed with pleasure. Once a week he dealt out oatmeal and potatoes to them in return for their services. They were content enough, for the crop had been a poor one and some of them served hard masters.

As he pushed open the front door of the Manse, the sound of children's voices came to his ears. The parlor door was ajar, the yellow candle-light came out into the darkness of the hall in a soft shaft. He pushed open the door. He had entered so quietly that Allison did not hear him. He stood regarding his family from the doorway. Allison sat upon the floor; her dark hair was ruffled: the short curls, having escaped from the coil at the back of her head, hung softly round her face. Jean stood behind her, both hands pressed over Allison's eyes. Alex was cumbrously concealing his plump person behind the upright piano. The baby David sat on the hearthrug, following the proceedings with his bright eyes. He held a string of amber beads in his chubby fist, which Hamish recognized as a gift he had once made to Allison. He had thought at the time that they were perhaps a trifle unsuitable, but their color had charmed him. He had certainly not bought them for a baby to fling about and gnaw with wet greedy gums.

Jean was screaming with excitement, nearly choking Allison in her desire to avoid all chance of Alex's being seen. Her dancing gray eyes suddenly caught sight of Hamish in the doorway; her hands dropped from Allison's eyes, and she said uncertainly, as though not sure whether she should speak at all: "Papa—here's Papa back very soon, Mama."

Allison started to her feet, blood rushing to her cheeks. Her hands flew involuntarily to her untidy hair.

"My dear," said Hamish coldly, "the noise the children are making is somewhat penetrating." He paused. "It is five o'clock, I believe," he continued, as though sorely perplexed at the presence of the children in the parlor at that hour. He turned to Jean. "Take your brother up to the nursery now."

Silently the child held her hand out to the little boy and together they left the room. The sound of their feet ascending the stairs was audible in the silence that followed, Alex laboriously climbing one step at a time.

Excuses and apologies flashed through Allison's mind—Bella had toothache, she had promised the children a treat, she was on the floor to prevent David's rolling into the fireplace—but she was too weary to produce them. She waited for him to speak; there was silence for a few moments while she stared at him.

"I cannot think, Allison, what has come over you lately," he said in a deep ministerial voice. "You know that it is not my wish that the children should romp about in the downstairs rooms; the nursery is, rather naturally, the place in which children should play; had you been reading to them or hearing them recite, it would have been a different matter." He paused, expecting her flood of apologies, a few tears he expected, and then he would forgive her. But she stood before him with that strange far-away look in her eyes, as though she had not heard what he said.

He was disconcerted, but he continued doggedly, "Either you have wilfully disobeyed me or wilfully deceived me." At this she moved her hand to her bosom and words came fluttering from her mouth, almost inaudible.

"Oh, no, Hamish, I—" She paused for a second. "I am very sorry."

His face softened and he stepped forward to kiss her. He put his arm around her shoulders and drew her to him.

She shrank from him and pushed him away with an almost hysterical gesture. Hamish fell back, his face pale with astonishment. He was more deeply hurt than ever before in his life. Allison hardly seemed to realize what she had done; she continued to watch him fascinated.

He turned and strode out of the room. As he passed the unfinished portrait, on an easel by the door, the eyes seemed to look out at him, with a kind of mocking joy. He crossed the hall and shut himself into the study.

Allison drew her hand across her forehead, then with a sigh she stooped down and picked up the baby from the hearthrug. A smile lit up her face as she saw his funny one-sided little grin, and heard his pleased chorus of sounds. Hamish had faded from her mind. She drew him close to her and kissed the dark fluffy down on the top of his head. As she carried him out through the door, her eyes also fell on the portrait, and the vacant dead look came into them again.

Later in the evening Allison sat alone in the parlor. Hamish had not come in for supper at half-past five. The baize door of his study had remained closed. Allison had sent Jean to ask him whether he would prefer his food to be brought to him. The child had pushed open the heavy swing door with difficulty. She stood just inside, afraid to speak. The lamplight fell on Hamish's bent head as he sat at his desk; the child thought he looked very stern as he raised his eyes.

"Well, child?" he said impatiently.

Jean did not speak, she only hung her head.

Hamish's much-tried patience was at an end. Was he some incredible monster that his wife shuddered at his touch, and his children dared not answer him when he spoke to them? His fist crashed down on the desk, scattering papers on the carpet.

"Come here!" he commanded angrily.

Jean advanced timidly, till she stood close to his desk; she fidgeted from one foot to another; her gray eyes filled with tears. Mechanically she stooped down and gathered the papers together with her tiny well-shaped hands.

"Stand up!" said Hamish.

The child obeyed, but she could not meet his penetrating gaze.

Hamish hated shiftiness. "What did you come for?" he asked sternly. "Answer me now at once!"

"Nothing," faltered the child; her mind was blurred with the terrible desire to escape to Allison and to leave this gloomy book-lined study.

Hamish was silent for a moment, then he said slowly:

"Jean, you are lying."

The child raised her horror-stricken eyes slowly. Why had she said what she did not mean? Why had she not delivered her mother's message? The tears blinded her; she rubbed her eyes desperately with her fist.

"Do you know what happens to children who lie?" inquired Hamish, leaning forward. There was no answer. "God is angry with them and will take care of them no longer; when they die the Devil takes them away to Hell to be punished forever in the fire." It seemed to ease his bitterness of heart to vent his rage and disturbance on this defenseless child. "Kneel down and pray God will forgive you."

The child fell upon her knees, hiding her wild frightened little face in her hands.

"Repeat the words after me," commanded Hamish. " 'O Lord, here before Thy throne I kneel, a miserable sinner, who seeks salvation through Thy everlasting mercy.' "

In a choked voice Jean echoed the words, stumbling over "salvation" and "everlasting" because her tongue was yet that of a baby.

Suddenly Hamish was sickened: the tiny child kneeling before him and he bullying and terrifying—the picture nauseated him.

"Go quickly!" he said angrily, and seizing her roughly by the shoulder he jerked her to her feet and sent her flying towards the door.

The child needed no second bidding; she fled across the dark hall and flung herself sobbing into the dining-room, where Allison sat alone in the candle-light.

For some time Allison could not understand what had happened; the child was frenzied with fear. The picture of a flaming Hell had been raised in her mind once more, and she clung to her mother with hot eager hands. When Allison had succeeded in quieting her she carried her upstairs and put her to bed herself, sitting beside the crib with the small hand clasped in hers till the child fell asleep.

As she stood gazing down on the flushed face,

life began to flow back into her veins again. For nearly two months, ever since Simon had gone, she had felt like something made of stone. Sometimes when she lay in bed at night, she let her brain travel in a weary circle. What could be the point of human existence? How was it that God was love, when the pain and sorrow in the world so outweighed the happiness? Why? Why anything? She supposed she must go on living on the earth because there were the meals to order, and Hamish's new shirts to make, and the house would get so dirty without her to see that everything was dusted and polished. Then there would be no one to sing to Hamish in the evening when he had finished his sermon, and—oh, there were countless other little odds and ends which were a barrier between her and death. She did not want to die, either—death was something horrid and unbelievable; but if she could just cease, if her life could be changed into some kind of dream which could dissolve like the early morning mist. At first the tortured face of Andrew Simon seemed always before her, with those deep smoldering eyes and the gentle mouth, twisted into an ironical sneer; it made her want to cry aloud; and the love that had burned

within him she had thrown away for what?
Why had she done it? What was the use of
married life without love? She knew now that
she did not love Hamish in any spiritual sense
of the word, neither did he attract her physically. She was used to him and admired him,
but that was all; she realized now that she had
never felt for him any of the agonizing bitter
sweetness of her love for Simon. But now, as
she stood looking down on the child, she seemed
to take a firmer grip on life again. This child
which she had brought into the world was flesh
of her flesh and bone of her bone. It was tied
to her with a strange bond which could never
be broken. A slow happiness began to creep
into her mind; very softly she tiptoed from the
room and went downstairs.

In the hall stood a young woman wrapped in
a tartan plaid. Her head was bowed, and Allison could hear her catch her breath in a sob.
Slowly she descended the stairs, the candle still
in her hand; her taffeta frock rustled as it swept
over the carpet.

At the bottom she paused, one hand on the
banisters.

"Can I help you?" she said gently. "Is it the
Minister you wish to see?"

The girl raised her head. She had a rugged, big-boned face, but there was great vitality and charm about it. Her eyes were that strange light blue which is often found in those of the Highland people; her hair straggled from beneath her plaid in fiery red wisps.

"My father is with the Minister now," she answered in the soft deliberate English of the Highlanders.

Allison recognized the girl as the Mairi McLeod who lived with her father and mother in the last croft but one, towards the southern headland. They were respectable and God-fearing people, and attended the kirk regularly, unlike many of their neighbors.

"But, Mairi, what's the matter?" insisted Allison, seeing the girl's distress. "Is your mother ill? What has happened?" She laid her hand on the girl's shoulder; she had almost to stand on tiptoe to do this. "My dear, don't cry like that. Tell me what I can do to help you?"

"It is not for the likes of you, Mistress McGregor, to hear my trouble," said Mairi in choked tones. "It'll be sending me away they'll be," she suddenly cried wildly, flinging up her head.

"But, Mairi, why? What is it that ails you?" reiterated Allison.

The other woman looked down into Allison's great dark eyes, so soft and worried; she saw the sweetness of her mouth and the youthfulness of her figure clad in the tightly fitting dress of lilac taffeta; she was the Minister's wife, but there was something about her as she stood there which put courage into the wretched girl.

"I am to have a child, and I am not a married woman," she said simply, in dull flat tones.

There was silence for a moment and then Allison said, unexpectedly—she did not know herself quite why she said it:

"Did you love the man who is your child's father?"

"Yes, I love him," answered the girl, raising her head with a hint of pride, "and I made him happy and I made myself happy and now—everything is unhappiness."

There were often cases of this kind which were brought to Hamish to judge, and to call sinners to repentance; it was a thing that disgusted him, he was hard with the delinquents.

At that moment the study door opened, and Hamish stood in the doorway. He called

Mairi by name; she advanced slowly and the door shut again.

Allison was left alone in the hall. She could hear Hamish's voice raised in denunciation. She did not move. Once or twice a word came through more clearly; she heard "corrupt," "uncleanly." Once his great beautiful voice boomed forth and she heard him cry in anger about "the murder of beauty."

Allison pressed her hands over her ears. How easily might she be kneeling before Hamish, while he stormed over her—if she were not untrue in deed, she was in mind, "the murderer of beauty." What beauty had she ever known, save during those few short months with Simon?

She hurried across the hall into the parlor, the blue smoke from the candle streaming outward in the darkness. The candles were lit and their mellow light fell on the unfinished portrait; the eyes smiled forth at her. Supposing she had let him finish it— A storm of misery overwhelmed her, she pressed the back of her hand to her forehead and closed her eyes. She forced herself to think of the children, of their thick curly heads and soft skin and their queer little voices.

Presently she felt calmer. Later she heard

the McLeods going; she longed to say a word of comfort to Mairi, but she did not dare go into the hall.

She heard the door bang and then Hamish came into the parlor; he looked tired and dispirited. He sat there in silence.

"What is it, my dear?" said Allison timidly.

"Oh, nothing that you could understand," he answered coldly and wearily; "only wickedness and ugliness and filth."

She moved over to the back of his chair, then she stooped and kissed him good-night. She felt ashamed of her conduct earlier in the evening. It was not Hamish's fault that Simon had gone away—forever—it was only the way things were; if only he did not touch her too much, then everything would be all right. He put his hand up to her bent head, and kissed her. His eyes were humble and imploring; he felt somehow that Allison was far away from him.

Chapter XVI

WINTER came very fast that year. There seemed to be only a brief golden period between the misty heat of summer and the bare blackness of winter. The rain came again, lashing ceaselessly at the windows, and there was always the sound of dripping, except when the wind was so high that it drowned everything in its overbearing onrush. The trees round the Manse, bending before the gale, inclined further toward the mountains; they were perpetually straining away from the sea as though they were afraid. There was snow on the mountain-tops very early, and great swirling banks of mist came hurrying down the slopes and then settled furtively in the clefts and glens.

The weather was so bad that Hamish spent much of his time in his study; he was engaged in writing a short history of Covenanting Times in Scotland. The darkness and the enforced sitting indoors depressed him; although he would not admit it to himself, he was worried about

Allison—even he had noticed the weariness in her face. She had seemed strange to him, and he had not forgotten the night when she had pushed him away, a violent repugnance in her gesture and expression. Doubts began to assail him once more. It was a year since he had come to Glenlee and everything that had seemed to him so important at the time seemed to have dwindled to nothing. What had he done, after all? Had he brought happiness to the people? Had he raised their idea of the good and the beautiful? Had he shown them God? True, he had improved things materially: the Poor Fund, the organized Session of Elders, the vaccination of the people, the presentation of Bibles, and now the new causeway, which would be of much use to them. All these things had been instituted by him.

As the winter had drawn in, and the weather was too bad to venture forth in fishing-smacks, and the few potatoes from the scanty crop had run out, the people were fed by means of the money that he had collected in London. But— "Man shall not live by bread alone." The gleam deep down in the eyes of these Highlanders was the same as it always had been; something primeval lurked in their minds, against which he could not combat. Once or twice it had leaped out at him, as on the occasion (which he had never forgotten) of the Desecration of the Lord's Supper—it figured in capital letters in his mind. Were they capable of a feeling for God which would uplift them?

In London he had spoken with many eminent men, and these conversations had set up a mental excitement which seemed totally unsuited to produce sermons for the inhabitants of Glenlee. He felt himself a prophet; he could have been a Covenanting Leader and died for his religion, but this continual labor to instil the spirit of God into—animals—seemed to drag his spirit downwards. He was shocked the first time that he thought of his people as animals, but the idea remained. Tracing these new ideas to their source, he discovered that it was Andrew Simon who had first spurred his mind into activity. It seemed to him as though Simon had taken a stick and stirred his mind round and round, so that new values appeared, and old ones sank to the bottom. Then he had gone to London: the vision of the first sail up the Thames and the sight of the Houses of Parliament came back to him. And now—he felt as though he were a prisoner, surrounded forever by the everlasting mists, seas and mountains.

It was in this mood that he began to notice the schoolmaster, McLellan, once more. For over four months the man had behaved with decency. He drank secretly, but he was no more seen staggering along the sea's edge as early as eleven o'clock in the morning. His appearance, although still wild, was slightly improved. His long gray hair had been trimmed, and the big round buttons on his coat polished. Hamish had been surprised to see him in the kirk once or twice, his fierce eyes gleaming beneath his thick eyebrows.

So it was that Hamish, returning one night from superintending the work on the causeway, spoke to McLellan for the first time for months.

It was a cold evening, and the darkness was falling very fast; a chilly unhappy wind moaned round the corners of the crofts with their rain-sodden thatch. The schoolhouse stood a little apart. McLellan was standing in the doorway as Hamish called out his "Good-night." The older man answered in his melodious voice. To-night he was quite sober.

"Will ye no come in for a moment, Minister?" he said.

Something in the stoop of his shoulders and the cold darkness of the schoolhouse touched Hamish. He stopped, pushed open the gate with his blistered hands, and followed McLellan inside.

The schoolmaster lived in two wretched rooms at the back of the big draughty school-room; a dark passage, smelling of mildew, led to them. He pushed open the door, which squeaked unpleasantly on its hinges. A candle was burning on the mantelpiece and two or three peats glowed in an isolated pile in the middle of a big fireplace. The ashes of many previous fires lay strewn about the hearth. There was a strange smell of peat smoke, musty leather and stale spirits. The tiny room was lined with volumes, thick with dust; a table in one corner bore the remains of a meal, dirty plates were piled in one corner. Beside the fire sat an old sheepdog who scratched himself ceaselessly, knocking his elbow against the bare boards.

Hamish wished he had not come: the atmosphere both physically and morally sickened him.

McLellan was usually ill-mannered in his intercourse with Hamish: his mouth would twist satirically at the sight of the younger man, laboring diligently at the new causeway, or hurrying through the wind and rain to visit a sick crofter, his Bible making an awkward bulge from an inside pocket.

To-night, however, he seemed in a strange mood; his eyes, still keen, though bleared by hard drinking, had a far-away look in them. He stretched his hand downward restlessly to fondle the dog's head. He talked rapidly all the time, and when Hamish made a move to go, he said quickly: "No, Minister, stay a while longer to oblige an old man," and indeed his voice sounded old and faint.

"It is many a day since I spoke with an educated man—'deed I have not been fit company —but sometimes the longing comes on me to talk with some one—for the men of Glenlee use me only as men use a necessary tool or a fishing-net. They use me to write letters for them, to add up money for them, but they do not talk with me. I am still a stranger to them although I have lived here among them more than thirty years. At one time the isolation was almost more than a man could stand. During the first years that I was here, many were the times I decided to send in my resignation, but somehow—it was never sent—and I am still here after thirty years." He smiled slowly, shaking his massive head. The Highland lilt had disappeared from his voice and he spoke in a low, mellow, cultured voice.

Hamish sat down once more. He was attracted by this new side of McLellan, a side of which he had never obtained a glimpse before.

"I wonder why you never went?" said Hamish slowly. "Was there nothing that you wished to do in the world, that you went on living in this dark schoolhouse year after year? Or was there no opportunity offered you?"

"Yes, opportunity came once or twice," replied McLellan. "I was offered a post in Glasgow, and later one near Aberdeen. I was once considered a good scholar—" He smiled at this, as though he were speaking diffidently of a son of his, or of a friend long dead.

"And you chose to stay here?" said Hamish in puzzled tones.

"I did not exactly choose," replied McLellan slowly. "You see it was—too late." He said the last few words with peculiar intensity, shooting a glance at Hamish from beneath his shaggy brows.

"I don't think I quite follow you," murmured

Hamish. There was something hypnotic about the man's eyes. Hamish felt as though he had no desire to speak, he only wished to listen. Usually conversation excited him into argument, and sometimes declamation, but to-night he did not wish to speak; perhaps it was because he was physically weary after a hard day's work on the causeway.

"When you have lived here a few more years, you will understand," continued McLellan. "Every winter the mist sweeps down to meet the sea, and Glenlee is cut off from the rest of the universe. A man becomes more and more alone, but the mist seems to sink into him until he is as nebulous as itself, he becomes part of it, he is encircled by it forever." Although he spoke in low tones there was a strange gleam in McLellan's long narrow eyes. Hamish moved uneasily in his seat; he had been certain when he entered that the man was sober, but now he was not so sure.

"In the end a man becomes so much a part of the mist that he cannot escape from it; and yet he is still a man, or what is left of a man; everything is taken from him, save the spirit of imagination. Determination, pride, energy, all give way before the ever-growing power of imagination—and this tortures the ghost that was once a balanced human being. What has a man in this position to look forward to? Only death illuminated by the power of imagination. What kind of companion is that for a man? Here in Glenlee there are hours and hours of immobility, when there is no other companion but one's own thoughts—one's wild fancies—when eternity and the universe seem to overwhelm and crush, when the world is reduced to an atom, and the creatures upon it less than dust. What kind of companions are those thoughts?"

The old man paused; the hand that caressed the dog's head trembled slightly.

Hamish was silent, carried away by this flood of eloquence. Dimly he grasped McLellan's meaning; a dread was dawning in his mind. This deadness, this immobility which he had noticed so often among the people of Glenlee, it was a menace to everything in which he believed.

McLellan continued more quietly: "When I first came here, I was a young man. I was a scholar. I was in my own way something of a poet. I was an idealist. I gloried in the idea that I should inspire the minds of these ignorant people with learning. For several years I worked like a madman. Then by degrees the energy began to go from me, I felt myself defeated by the strangeness of the people. Sometimes they seemed hardly human, as though they knew of things I did not and were incapable of realizing an ideal such as I had set up before me."

Hamish shifted uneasily once more, glancing at the dusty square of window through which he could see the dark blue of the early darkness. This strange, despicable creature with his wild eyes, why was he framing in words the thoughts which Hamish had attempted to banish from his own mind as unworthy of it? A growing horror of the future began to overwhelm him.

"Sometimes I cannot bear my loneliness," said McLellan in very low tones, "and so I try to—forget it—by drinking myself into unconsciousness."

There was silence in the room for several seconds. Suddenly the old man sank his head on his hand and a harsh dry sob cut through the stillness.

"At times," he faltered, "I feel myself to be the man I was twenty or thirty years ago, and

I try to regain pride and decency—as now—but loneliness will not leave me alone; I am tortured. I cannot bear it. Once more I must seek comfort in oblivion. It is always the same, I—I am a dead man." His voice broke, and he remained with his head sunk in his hands.

They sat in silence for a minute or two, then Hamish rose. He ought to say something, point out to the suffering man that there was comfort in God, that he must be strong; but no words would come. He was appalled, terrified, shaken out of his customary calm. He laid his hand gently on McLellan's shoulder and then let himself out into the frosty night.

The old man did not move.

The sky was a clear blue; silhouettes of the blunted thatched roofs of the crofts stood out against its clearness, thick and richly dark. The sound of his feet echoed in the silence with a metallic ring, as he hurried past the dimly lit windows. The dust of the schoolhouse seemed to cling to him. The steeps of Ben Buie towered above him; the banks of white mist glinted strangely in the moonlight. The road wound upwards, showing white here and there, then it seemed to fade into the mist. He

turned once as he ascended the hill. The sea
was dark and restless; the moonlight fell on
the gravestones and the kirkyard wall standing
silently above the faintly moving water. Everything seemed to lower vastly around him; there
was no outlet. McLellan's words echoed in his
mind, "I am a dead man—I am a dead man."

As he stood in the dark, stone-flagged hall of
the Manse, he heard the thin note of the piano
coming from the parlor, and then the soft
rounded notes of Allison's voice. Music had
always the power to soothe him; he stood silent
and listened. Gently the words came to him:

> "Thou'll break ma heart, thou bonnie bird
>   That sings beside thy mate;
>   For sae I sat, and sae I sang,
>   And wist na o' my fate."

The sadness of the song brought quick tears
to his eyes; he entered the parlor quietly. The
candles cast a soft glow over Allison as she sat
at the piano; her soft dark head was bowed; but
as he entered she raised her face, and he saw
that tears shone on her lashes. She rose to greet
him dutifully.

"Why, how cold you are!" she said, drawing
him towards the fire which blazed in the grate,

but it was newly lit and did not give off much heat. Hamish had a passion for economy in peat and coals: sometimes Allison was so cold that she had to keep moving about the house.

He sat down in one of the hard horsehair chairs and spread out his large, shapely hands to the yellow tongues of flame.

"My dear, play something for me," he said complacently.

"My hands are cold, Hamish," she answered quickly; "the fire has only just been lit—I—I am not in the mood for playing to-night."

He glanced up, surprised. She stood before him tugging at a tiny handkerchief which she held between her fingers. She looked pale and tired; in six months' time she would bear him his fourth child, therefore he was ever gentle with her. He spoke persuasively, so that presently she moved over to the instrument once more and sat down at the keyboard. She fluttered the leaves of the Burns' Song Book, out of which she had been playing. Then the silence was broken and the little instrument rang out in fierce remonstrating chords. As though strained to breaking-point:

"The bonniest lad that e'er I saw
Bonnie laddie, Highland laddie—"

When she had finished there was a pause.
Hamish rose and came over to the lighted instrument; he turned over the pages of the music
and settled them for her, one hand on her
shoulder. He could feel that she was trembling; he wondered idly what could ail her,
women were queer at these times. He slid his
hand forward over her warm rounded breast.
Quickly she leaned forward and began to play,
her voice trembling slightly as she sang his favorite song:

> "When o'er the hills the eastern star
>   Tells bughtin-time is near, my Jo,
> And owsen frae the furrow'd field
>   Return sae dowf and wearie O!"

He was conscious of the music, but by the
second verse his thoughts were elsewhere. He
would write at once to his influential friends
in Edinburgh—perhaps there was a chance of a
ministry coming vacant there; he would stay no
longer encircled by mist and sea. The vision of
McLellan's bowed head came before his eyes
again, and he banished it at once. What pretty
hands Allison had!

> "I'll meet thee on the lea-rig,
>   My ain kind dearie O!"

She sang on. At the end he thanked her and then went across to his study to write to Edinburgh.

Allison sat where he had left her, gazing before her. After a minute or two she rose quickly and hurried upstairs to the nursery. There she drew the children round her and heard them laugh and felt the clutch of their eager hands.

Chapter XVII

THE winter that year was long and bitter, it seemed as though the spring would never come again. The rain was terrific, and the winds had been unceasing and tempestuous. but out of doors the immobility was gone. There was ceaseless noise and the wind scattered the terrified last year's leaves. All day the thundering of the waves could be heard up at the Manse. Inside the house, doors creaked and swung to and fro, the carpets rose with the draught, and the curtains moved. The sharp attack of hail on the windows could be heard above the roar of the wind.

At the end of February Hamish was called to Edinburgh to preach before a congregation. There were three candidates for a vacant parish there. His hopes flamed high; he saw himself in the world, leading great legions of men; he was remote always, in a kind of dream.

On the second day after he had gone, Allison was sitting alone in the parlor writing a letter to her sister in her graceful pointed hand.

There seemed nothing to say nowadays. Was anything of real interest? What did anything matter to her sister far away in the southern Dumfries?

My dear Agnes,
I am well and was much pleased by your last letter. Hamish is at present from home preaching in Edinburgh.

A hair stuck on her quill. Slowly she picked it out, raising her eyes to the rain-dimmed window. In the corner stood the unfinished portrait with its happy eyes.

There was a sound at the door, it was pushed open, and Jean came in. The child walked as though blind, with one small hand stretched out before her. She whimpered slightly. In a second Allison was on her knees beside her, a fear clutching at her heart. The child dropped her head against Allison's shoulder and closed her large gray eyes; her face was flushed.

"What is it, Jeanie? What is it?" whispered Allison in an agony. The strange stillness of the little body frightened her.

"I'm so tired, Mama," she murmured almost inaudibly. "My head is all aches." She drew a weary hand across her brow.

Allison picked her up and carried her to the nursery. The grim Bella sat by the window sewing; she always sat there like some piece of statuary that belonged to the room, as the mantelpiece or window-ledges did. Together they put the child to bed and John was sent on Paddy to fetch Dr. Fraser from Strathnairn.

Jean did not speak again for some hours; the fever seemed to be growing on her. She tossed and turned and a hectic flush mounted to her brow. She moaned sometimes as though in pain.

Dr. Fraser arrived about six o'clock. He was old and tired, and the sight of the child bewildered and troubled him. He applied leeches to her brow, but he was puzzled; he shook his head. Allison stood on the other side of the bed, white and strained. Her mind framed the question, "What is it?" but her lips would not move. She looked across at the old man mutely. He seemed to understand her, for he shook his head and said, "I canna say, Mistress McGregor, I canna say, but I have a fear in me that it might be the water in the head."

Allison looked at the bright head on the pillow, with its thick bush of fair reddish curls;

everything seemed incredible, fantastic; she looked at the doctor once more with unseeing beautiful eyes.

"Will she live?" she said slowly.

"I canna say," replied the old man gently; "in the morning I shall be able to tell more certainly."

He left many instructions and drove off in his gig. He would be there the first thing in the morning again.

At nine o'clock Jean opened her wide gray eyes and spoke suddenly. She had been dreaming and crying out in her sleep. Sometimes it was "Fergus McGeachy," and sometimes "the flames" and "the great black hole" or the "cupboard" and the Shorter Catechism. It broke Allison's heart to hear her, but now she was quite calm.

"Mama, what is the matter?" she said bewildered, turning appealing eyes to Allison.

"Why, my darling, you're not well just now, but soon you'll be better," whispered Allison, stroking the soft hair away from the brow.

"I shan't die, Mama, shall I?" faltered the child, terror coming into her eyes.

"Why, my precious, no, you'll be well very soon," said Allison gently.

"When shall I be well? When? When?" insisted Jean. "Shall I be well to-morrow?"

"Why, perhaps, my darling," murmured Allison. "Go to sleep and don't worry at all, my sweet."

"Sing, Mama, sing to Jeanie," demanded the child.

Softly Allison sang:

"Oh can ye sew cushions and can ye sew sheets,
  And can ye sing ba-la-loo when the bairnie greets."

What should she do—she could not even face the thought of the child's death, but the doctor had said that she might not live—what would Hamish say? The child must be prepared for Heaven—prepared to meet her Maker— Then anger seized her. What other state could she be in, this beautiful innocent? Her voice faltered, but she sang on.

Suddenly the child was taken with a violent shivering fit, and then she lay very still, one arm twitching convulsively. She muttered and screamed with fright—it was always the flames and Satan. Once she tried to rise in bed to ward something off, but she could not move. One side seemed paralyzed. She did not recognize Allison or understand what she said. Tum-

bled words of Psalms came pouring forth, and
then there was piteous sobbing because the poor
little brain could not find some evading line.

Once she laughed and held out one little
hand.

"Oh, Mama—come quick and look at this
pretty, twirly shell." Then her hand fell once
more and she screamed in fear and loneliness.

At a quarter past twelve she died, this joyous
and beautiful little creature that had seemed
immortal. Allison's brain was numbed. Bella
led her away from the bedside; the tears were
streaming down the elder woman's face, but
Allison was dry-eyed; it seemed as though all
this had happened to some one else. She would
open her eyes and find herself awake again.
The quiet little body lying peacefully on the
bed was nothing but a sleeping child. In the
morning Jean would move again and come
dancing in to wake her.

Hamish returned two days later. It had been
impossible to let him know the news. Allison
stood down by the sea and watched the ship
which was bringing him home, tacking backwards and forwards as it rounded the corner.
It was early afternoon, but already the sun was
sinking, flooding the sea with crimson. All the

unbearable moments of her life seemed connected with the wayward beauty of ships driven before the wind, appearing and disappearing behind dark points of land. She watched the rowing boat approach the land slowly; idly she saw a heavy gull silhouetted against the evening light as it stood on one leg on a rock at the sea's edge.

Hamish sprang ashore eagerly, and hurried up the shelving beach to meet her. He held his tall black hat in his hand, and his gray eyes gleamed with triumph and pleasure. He had preached well, he was filled with confidence, he no longer drank in the beauty of the hills with painful ecstasy, his mind was filled with eager hopes and intoxicated by the thought of a vast congregation sitting under him, all silent and attentive, stirring slightly as his voice rose in excitement.

Allison moved mechanically to meet him. He grasped her cold hands in his and kissed her on the forehead. She spoke in low flat tones the words she had been rehearsing, "Jeanie is dead." They meant nothing to her; during those two days she had never fully realized the child's death, her brain was too stunned to grapple with the terrifying "forever."

Hamish stopped, his face ludicrously blank. The light died from his face.

"But, Allison, how—?" His voice was husky.

In emotionless tones she recited the details as they walked slowly up the hill. When he reached the Manse, Hamish hurried to the room where the child lay. Allison stood on the opposite side of the bed; her eyes sought the window. She would not look on the frozen stillness. She knew that he was suffering greatly, but he seemed utterly remote from her. He drew in his breath sharply. She tore her gaze from the window. His eyes were full of tears and his mouth was working.

"The Lord has given, and the Lord has taken away; blessed be the name of the Lord!" A pitiful glow of faith lit up his handsome features. He fell on his knees beside the bed and prayed.

Silently Allison went away, downstairs to the parlor. She was unmoved. Somewhere deep within her she ached for his anguish, but the feeling was swamped by this cold deadness and bewilderment. What was the Lord to do with Jeanie? She was gone forever; reality had gone with her, all the rest was fantastic, a mere dream.

On the following Monday night, David the baby whimpered continually. After several hours he fell into a heavy troubled sleep which afterwards developed into a kind of torpor. He slept through the next day and late on the following night he died.

No one knew the exact moment of his death. Bella was sitting sewing in the corner of the nursery; this was the second night of watching. Her head had nodded as she listened to the stertorous heavy breathing of the young child. When she woke she was conscious of something missing. The silence seemed to be beating in her ears. Then she knew what it was. She hurried to the crib. The tiny dark head was thrown back, the mouth was slightly open, but no breath came from between the lips. She stood silent for a minute, like some quaint statue, then she turned and hastened to Allison's bedroom, where she had gone to snatch an hour or two's rest. She knocked on the door and entered.

Allison was awake at once; her nerves seemed strained to breaking-point. She sat up in the dark four-poster, her dark eyes shadowed with weariness, her face dead white beneath her tumbled dark hair.

"What is it, Bella?" she whispered. "Is he worse?"

The old woman advanced to the bedside and laid her hard, toil-worn hand on Allison's, where it rested outside the coverlet.

"He's awa' to the Lord," she said simply, the gentle reverence of her tones imbuing the odd hard words with beauty.

For a moment Allison did not move. She sat there gazing at the older woman as she stood holding the candle aloft. Then, very slowly, she turned and shook Hamish by the shoulder. He was a heavy sleeper and his soft even breathing continued undisturbed for some time. Then he moved restlessly and finally opened his eyes.

Allison did not speak for a moment. Bella had left the room and the candle stood on the pedestal by the bedside. Then, as Hamish sat up sleepily, she turned to him and said: "Hamish, David is dead too, David and Jean, they're both dead." She seemed to be trying to persuade herself into believing the unbelievable. Hamish gave her a bewildered, horrified look and began to climb slowly out of bed. She followed him quietly along the passage to the nursery. She was not thinking of anything;

it was strange how Hamish's white heels stuck out of his shoes where he had trodden down the backs. His white nightshirt caught against the banisters on the landing.

In the nursery the fire was still burning, the cot was drawn up to the hearth. In the far corner Alex slept peacefully, one chubby hand thrown out over the coverlet.

As they stood over the cot, Allison began to realize the import of the words, "David is dead." She touched the little cheek, and the coldness and immobility that met her there filled her with terror. She shrank from the child. This was not David, her child, but something horrible, overwhelmingly terrifying.

David indeed was dead.

Hamish, his face soft with pity, knelt down and prayed by the cot. Allison knelt down also, but she did not pray: it seemed to her a useless thing to do. David and Jean were gone, disappeared like the light of a candle. Of course she knew they were in Heaven with the Lord, because she had been told of Heaven and Hell so often, but this knowledge did not seem real, not part of the knowledge that told her that Jean's dolls still lay in the corner of the nursery and would not be wanted any more.

A movement from Alex's crib in the corner
made her look up. The child was turning over
in his sleep. A sudden terror assailed her.
What if Alex should die, too? She rose to her
feet desperate, and broke into Hamish's devo-
tions sharply.

"Hamish, carry Alex through to our bedroom; he cannot stay here with—with this."
She could not bring herself to call the dead
child "David."

"In a moment, my dear," said Hamish,
frowning in spite of his pity for her.

"No, now, now!" insisted Allison, as though
she were warding off Death, as though she felt
his overwhelming presence in the room. Silently he obeyed, lifting the warm, sleeping
child in his arms. As Allison followed him she
glanced once more at the cot by the hearth; she
caught a glimpse of the little dark head lying
as though asleep. She closed her eyes and red-
hot flames seemed to leap up in her mind and
overwhelm her. She crept along the passage
back to the heavy four-poster bed. Alex lay in
the crook of Hamish's arm, pressed against his
side. She lay down quietly beside him, then
suddenly she started up once more and shook
Hamish by the shoulder.

"We must send him away at once, Hamish, out of this terrible house."

"My dear, whom shall we send away?" said Hamish, startled.

"Why, Alex, of course," she said hurriedly, the words tumbling over one another. "We must send him away to my sister Jane's—anywhere, so long as he goes from here."

Hamish tried to calm her, and would give no promise to send the child away. He felt that he could not bear to be separated from him; he drew him close to his side.

"The Lord is merciful, my dear," he said.

With a stifled sob Allison turned over and lay still in the darkness. For the first time since Jean's death, heavy tears poured down her cheeks as though nothing would stop them. She stretched out her hand so that she might feel Alex's little body.

Ten days later Alex died, smitten by the same terrible paralysis that had killed his brother and sister.

Chapter XVIII

ON the Sabbath following Alex's funeral, Hamish preached a sermon that was remembered by the people of Glenlee long after he had left them and had become an eminent divine in Edinburgh.

It was the first week in April and a bright blustery day. The sky was a perfect dazzling blue above the sharp crags of Scurr Dubh and Ben Buie. An occasional pure white cloud bloomed slowly and was then borne almost imperceptibly across the heavens. As Allison walked down the glen road towards the church, two buzzards hovered above the sky-line; she could see the bar on their wings, the wind was so strong that it swept them sideways along the tops of the crags. Now and again their strange unexpected cries came to her. As she crossed the bridge, the water thundered beneath, tossing and churning, so that the spray leaped up and was blown into her face. She watched it as it swept off a great rounded rock in a foam-decked amber stream. She stood there fasci-

nated, gazing over the rough parapet of the
bridge. In the distance the ugly clang of
the church-bell broke into the symphony of the
water and the wind.

Allison was dressed in black with white at
the throat and wrists. She wore a three-
cornered shawl with a fringe which fluttered
in the wind. Her cheeks were flushed, for the
morning, although bright, had a tang of frost
about it; but there were dark circles beneath
her eyes, and the eyes themselves were tragic:
she looked as though she might drop for very
weariness. She held a little silver-clasped Bible
close to her breast, clutching her shawl to her.
She had not wanted to go to church. Hamish
had been both hurt and astonished. He did
not know that she could not bear to see the
green salt-soaked churchyard where the three
children lay; she could not look at the grass
and clay without thinking of the rotting wood
of the coffins beneath. In the end she had
acquiesced; she had nothing left within her with
which to resist.

She hurried across the churchyard, followed
by curious and sympathetic eyes. She entered
the gloomy little church where the damp
crawled down the walls. A few people were

already seated as she hurried towards the little pew beneath the pulpit, her eyes cast on the ground before her.

Presently the men, who had been gossiping in the churchyard, came in, their heavy boots crunching on the stone flags. There was the patter of feet as one or two collies followed their masters, and lay down quietly beside the pews. All the people were peasants except for the factor's wife, Mrs. Fraser, in the pew opposite the one in which Allison sat. The laird's pew was empty. There was seldom any one in it. The laird himself had Parliamentary ideas and was nearly always absent in London. Meantime his factor bought up all the small holdings for sheep grazing, and the wretched inhabitants were left with no means of sustenance save that of fishing. Gradually they starved and the flood of emigration continued which had been depopulating the Highlands for years.

The younger women had plaids over their heads, while the older ones still wore the mutch. The men had their homespun plaids slung over their shoulders and most of them had old and tattered bonnets in their hands.

As Allison looked round the assembly in a

dull way, she noticed how the light from the narrow windows streamed onto the white mutches and the bowed gray heads of the men.

When the Beadle had preceded Hamish with the Bible, and when Hamish had prayed and finally ensconced himself comfortably in the pulpit, with the heavy Bible on his left and the odd notes for his sermon on the right, the congregation stood up to sing a Psalm. The note was given from an appointed place at the back of the church, and slowly and solemnly the metrical version poured forth like a ceaseless funeral dirge. Allison could hear Hamish's voice above all the others, as he stood above her in the pulpit. His black gown enhanced his great stature, and the light from the window fell upon his face and massive head. It pained her to see the sadness in his face; she thought to herself that he was made for triumph; the blazing gray eyes and proud mouth seemed made for greatness. As he sang, the sadness passed from his face.

> "Yea, though I walk in death's dark vale,
>   Yet will I fear no ill,
>   For thou art with me, and thy rod
>   And staff me comfort still."

He was aware that the eyes of the congregation were on him; the histrionic power which seldom deserted him helped him now to face the ordeal before him, for his heart was indeed sore. He had chosen the Psalms and paraphrases with great care. It helped him to see the tears creep down the toil-worn rugged cheeks of the congregation, just as it helped him to go into the nursery and finger the little pea-gun with which Alex had played. Sorrow was a dismal thing when there was no one to share it.

To Allison the service was agony. Her young, rounded face was set like stone. Again and again the same thought ran through her head. The children are gone, suddenly swept away like pollen in the wind, everything is finished. The fact had to be faced, it existed, then why smother the reality in all the strange ideas which seemed to her to have no connection with the fact? She was a pathetic figure as she stood there in her black bonnet and shawl, her head held proudly, her gentle mouth shut in a hard line. A longing for Andrew overwhelmed her once or twice, so that she drew in her underlip with her teeth. She had wanted him so desperately the last few weeks; but there had been no word from him since he had left. He had vanished almost as the children had. Everything she did seemed misinterpreted. Hamish was gentle with her, but he was hurt because she would not pray, and bewildered because she would not weep. He could not understand her, this hard, dry-eyed Allison—she had always seemed to him so gentle, so soft-hearted.

Hamish had chosen his text from the Book of Revelation. There was a fluttering of pages as the congregation found the text.

"What are those which are arrayed in white robes? And he said unto me, These are they which came out of great tribulation, and have washed their robes and have made them white in the blood of the Lamb."

Allison strove to believe in the perfect bliss of the children in Heaven, but it was all so unreal, so fantastic; only Jean screaming with fright, and the quiet little dark head of David were real. ". . . which came out of great tribulation. . . ." The angry face of Andrew rose before her with his dark cynical eyes. From what tribulation had these children escaped? She thought she was going to faint. The church whirled round her. She closed her eyes. She did not hear the rest of Hamish's sermon, but she knelt down mechanically to pray after he had finished, and she rose obediently with bowed head to receive the Blessing.

She saw Mrs. Fraser rise and leave the church, the feathers in her bonnet nodding grotesquely in their purple and red over those high rouged cheeks. She knew that she would be waiting in the churchyard, full of condolences. She had to summon all her fortitude to walk out of the church; her knees were trembling beneath her.

Mrs. Fraser was leaning out of her shabby carriage at the churchyard gate; she insisted upon taking Allison home. Under the rouge and the feathers there was kindness as well as curiosity. She talked incessantly all the way up the hill to the Manse, holding Allison's small hand in her own large bony one. She regaled her with stories of the elevated deceases and diseases of various relations of hers. Mrs. Fraser liked Allison; she felt she could patronize her without fear of a snub, Allison was too gentle to have a critical mind like some other ladies of her acquaintance. She was truly sorry for her now, and much elevated by what she called Hamish's "noble oration." She felt that a few more tears would be fitting on such an occasion; she shed several into a scented pocket-handkerchief.

Allison listened patiently, but the real meaning of the words did not reach her; she was feeling sick and the earth was spinning round her.

"So Mr. Simon is gone," babbled Mrs. Fraser, still clinging to Allison's hand. "I am sure you must miss him vastly—you and your husband." Mrs. Fraser had watched Allison walking on more than one occasion with Andrew; she had seen them sail down the sound the day of the picnic to Loch Doul; her curiosity had been aroused and then Andrew had unaccountably disappeared. Mrs. Fraser was baffled.

"I suppose the portraits were finished; indeed I should like to see them immensely," she continued, and then remembering the affliction under which the Manse was laboring she hurriedly added, "Later on, of course, when time has healed the aching wound." She was rather proud of this phrase, it sounded to her like a line from a hymn.

White as death, Allison lay back in the carriage.

"Why, my dear!" cried Mrs. Fraser, full of concern. "You are like a ghost. Whip up the horses, John."

The creaking carriage bumped and rumbled up the hill, the broken-winded horses wheezing under the strain of such unaccustomed speed. Allison gripped the worn leather seat to stop her from crying out. In places the horsehair was bursting out from the seat in ungainly tufts.

Mrs. Fraser assisted her out of the carriage at the Manse, and between them Bella and she undressed her and put her to bed. Allison's pains had begun. At half-past nine that evening, after a dangerous and difficult labor, she was delivered of a son, a tiny seven months' child.

Hamish had been almost beside himself all the afternoon and evening; his world seemed to be crashing about his ears. If Allison should die, he felt that he could not go on. He realized now as he had never realized before what uncomplaining courage she had. He saw her again stooping over the fire in the Neabost Inn, he saw her with flaming gallant eyes facing the drunken mob in the barn.

He wandered about the house like a lost soul. In the parlor her eyes smiled at him from the unfinished portrait, in his study her embroidery lay in the chair opposite his own, where she had forgotten it. The piano was open and the hymn-book lay on the top. He supposed she had left it ready for family worship in the evening. At the other end of the piano lay the Burns' Song Book. He thought of the night when she had sung to him.

He was not allowed to see her till the morning. He was shocked by her appearance, so frail and white did she look beneath the dark red canopy of the four-poster. The room was unbearably hot—Bella did not approve of fresh air either for the newborn baby or the newly delivered mother. The child was tiny, and he scarcely dared look at it, so delicate did it appear. He touched its cheek with the tip of his finger. A thrill ran through him and his eyes brightened. He was only young; he had been chastised by sorrow, but now he would triumph, his children should yet inherit the earth. For the first time since Jean's death he became impatient because he had heard nothing from Edinburgh. Would he receive a call or not?

With shining eyes he turned to Allison. She saw something in them that had not been there when he had gazed at her—was it only fourteen months ago—when David had been born. A reverential trust seemed to gleam from them, a pitiful belief in her. She gave him her little hand and smiled. He saw that her eyes were tranquil; she knew now partly why she could not leave him when every fiber of her being had cried out to her to go. With all his strength, he needed her.

Allison recovered slowly from the birth of her fourth child, Barnabas. Hamish had insisted on the name. The Son of Consolation. The baby thrived, but was a tiny delicate creature. During the terrible hours of her labor Allison seemed to have thrown something from her, the crushing, overpowering weight of her grief for her children, and her aching desire for Andrew's presence seemed to leave her, as she lay there, and gradually she grew able to think of both the children and Andrew. At one time her thoughts had fled like terrified birds every time she had turned them in the direction of these unescapable horrors. She felt calmer now; she watched a shadow of green in the trees outside burst into buds with a warmth that she had thought would never return to her.

The child Barnabas gave her pleasure—she loved the feel of the soft down on his tiny head. Something, however, had gone from her forever; part of her, which had been tortured and twisted when Andrew went, and then torn to pieces when she saw her children lying cold and strange in their cots, had given way with the strain, and fallen dead. Where that part had been was a dull ache, but the rest of her lived on.

She pitied Hamish. How odd, she thought, that would have sounded a year ago. He was so confident of himself and of God, and sometimes so childishly disappointed and infuriated by tiny things that did not matter.

The baby she loved, but the part of her that had worshiped her other children, that had made her feel through them the glory of the world, was dead. The child was a child, to be cared for and treated gently, that was all.

Her face seemed to have lost its roundness and with it part of the timid childishness which Andrew had loved so much. She was now a beautiful woman with deep sad eyes, where before she had been little more than a sensitive child. She no longer wept when Hamish remonstrated with her for being late with his meals.

Ten days after Barnabas was born Hamish had received his call to Edinburgh. They were to leave Glenlee the following November. His joy knew no bounds; he was arrogant, dogmatic, filling the house with his voice, but she knew that it was only for the moment—he would need her calmness and sympathy again soon enough. She was glad that he was happy again. Sometimes he was ashamed of himself because the melancholy caused by the death of the children had not persisted. He would go and gaze at the plain granite stone in the graveyard.

To

THE CHILDREN OF

THE REV. HAMISH QUENTIN McGREGOR,

OF GLENLEE.

DIED 1833.

JEAN, AGED SIX YEARS.

DAVID, AGED ONE YEAR.

ALEXANDER, AGED FOUR YEARS.

Tears would creep down his cheeks, but joy would flood his heart again at the sight of Barnabas sleeping peacefully in his cot, the watchful Bella always in attendance.

"The Lord is of great mercy," he would murmur.

And so in November they left Glenlee for

the gray streets of Edinburgh, and the blue
haar coming up from the Forth. As Allison
looked back down the glen, half-hidden from
view by swirling mist, an aching sadness which
had lurked at the back of her mind during the
last days swept down upon her in full force.
There were parts of Glenlee upon which she
could never look without a cruel stirring of
emotion—the copse with the whin bushes behind the house where once the children's voices
had broken the silence—and McAllister's croft
by the sea's edge, where she had seen Andrew
stand so often in the faint light of the gloaming. Nevertheless, the spirit of the place seemed
to have entwined itself into her being. It was
always there whenever she thought deeply. She
saw the wet leaves and heard the sound of the
sea and the water falling into the linn when
she thought of death. When she thought of
joy, somewhere in the back of her mind lurked
the vision of the silver wrinkled water and the
Islands far away on the blue horizon.

During the last two years life seemed to have
been shown to her with a height, depth and
color of which she had never dreamed before.
All the bitterness and joy of existence had been
revealed to her, and now the mist was closing

slowly. The Manse, with its eager prick-eared chimneys, disappeared at last and the side of Ben Buie was piled with tumbled clouds. Presently the sound of the sea died away; there was silence save for the crunch of the gig wheels on the rough stones, and the steady clip-clop of the horse's hooves.

Somewhere behind the mist the little square house still stood, and would stand, long after she and Hamish lay beneath the ground. Perhaps the house was the reality, and the people who had dwelt between its walls were ghosts, dissolving into nothingness, as though they had never been; as Andrew and the children had vanished, and as Hamish and she were doing at the moment. The mist thickened behind them.

She bowed her head in silence. She felt the eager hands of Jean about her neck and she saw once again the child dancing in the sun with the lilac blossom in her hand. Then again she saw the dark hazel eyes of Andrew as he kissed her on the shores of Loch Doul, gay wild eyes, cynical and sad by turns.

"When we reach Edinburgh—" Hamish was saying. She turned and gave him her attention.

EPILOGUE

ALLISON saw Andrew once again. It was seventeen years later. The day was blustery, and gusts of biting wind tore up from the Forth, whistling through the side roads and rushing across George Street. Allison was struggling along George Street. The wind had seized the ribbons of her bonnet and the fringe that hung from the sleeves of her little gray jacket. It tossed her voluminous skirts in every direction; vainly she pressed them to her side with her one free hand. She held a basket on her arm; she had been visiting some sick children and now the basket was empty.

At first appearance it seemed as though seventeen years had dealt with her lightly. Her face was still round and her hair dark. The gray in it was so slight that no one noticed it but herself. She still had the same gentle eyes and mouth. On closer inspection, however, a weariness had come into her face that had not been there in the Glenlee days; there were tiny wrinkles in her soft skin; her eyes regarded the world steadily, bravely, there was no fluttering timidity in them as of old. Her figure had thickened, she had borne six more children to Hamish since the birth of Barnabas, but she still walked with the same grace, and the tilt of her head had a pathetic hint of childishness in it even now when she looked up suddenly.

He was coming towards her down George Street, holding on his tall biscuit-colored hat with his right hand. In his left he held a black, silver-headed cane. She saw that his limp was as pronounced as of old. He was very smartly dressed, his royal-blue coat with its brass buttons so tightly waisted that he appeared almost feminine; his fawn trousers were strapped beneath his pointed boots; his waistcoat was bright, and he wore a large, dazzling white cravat. Something of the Eighteen-thirties seemed to cling to him, even perhaps of the gay Regency period. He was a little out of place with his bright waistcoat and brass buttons and his royal-blue coat in the Eighteen-fifties. He seemed old now. She noticed with a shock that his hair had gone very gray; he wore the short side-whiskers of an earlier fashion; his hazel eyes seemed darker than ever beneath the gray eyebrows. The lines at the corner of his eyes, and from nostril to mouth, were deeply engraven.

So the fashionable world had claimed him once more; but even as she thought this she saw him pause before a bookshop window. She halted in the side street, and watched him as he fingered the books. Presently he pushed his hat onto the back of his head; she saw again the unruly hair beneath. He read a page or two from some book, and then threw it down on the stall, impatient of its contents. She heard him ejaculate angrily, and as he turned to pursue his way she saw the light in his eyes again, and the amused cynical twist of his lips.

She slipped into the doorway as he crossed the street. She could not speak to him—after all these years she could not speak! He limped past the doorway without a sideways glance; a little further on he halted and she heard him hail a hackney. At the sound of that imperious husky voice, her heart almost seemed to stop beating. Then the hackney rattled off and she was left alone in the wind at the corner.

THE END